NOW DEAD IS ANY MAN

The discovery of a murdered body in the River Seine bring M. Pinaud into conflict with Conrad Roche, the rich and ruthless financier. Roche's methods of trying to stop the investigation unexpectedly turns the conflict into a vendetta, which lends an added excitement to the swiftly-moving suspense and the unexpected yet logical climax.

NOW DEAD IS ANY MAN

NOW DEAD IS ANY MAN

by
PIERRE AUDEMARS

MAGNA PRINT BOOKS
Long Preston, Yorkshire,
England.

British Library Cataloguing in Publicaton Data

Audemars, Pierre
  Now dead is any man.—Large print ed.
  I. Title
  823'.914(F)   PR6051.U3

  ISBN 0-86009-404-9

First Published in Great Britain by John Long Ltd

Published in Large Print 1982 by arrangement with Hutchinson
Publishing Group Ltd London and Walker & Company New York

Photoset in Great Britain by
Dermar Phototypesetting Co. Long Preston, Yorkshire.

Printed in Great Britain by
Redwood Burn Limited, Trowbridge, Wiltshire and
bound by Pegasus Bookbinding, Melksham, Wiltshire.

To
Caroline
for the grace of that
kindness, sympathy and
understanding she always
brings with her.

Any man's death diminishes me,
because I am involved in Mankind.
John Donne: *Devotions*

CHAPTER 1

In the days when M. Pinaud had come to the evening of his life he often took an innocent and perfectly understandable pleasure in recalling some of the more interesting and difficult cases which had crowded his brilliant and adventurous career.

As for example, his dealings with Conrad Roche, the financier.

The case really started—although at the time he did not know it—the same day he actually met this entirely ruthless, immensely powerful and completely unscrupulous criminal, when, just as he was thinking of going out to his modest lunch, he was peremptorily summoned by M. le Chef to that beautiful office on the first floor.

The great man looked up at him from behind his lovely ormolu desk with an air of vague bewilderment, as if having difficulty in remembering who he was and what he wanted.

M. Pinaud waited patiently in front of him, standing rigidly to attention, since the whole exquisitely furnished room possessed only one chair, and that was behind the desk, his massive weight forcing the soles and heels of his heavy boots deeper and deeper into the luxurious pile of the magnificent Aubusson carpet.

He did not say anything. He just waited, with infinite patience. He knew very well that this was only a pose—propaganda put over so often that the habit had become an addiction, which engendered its own momentum and hence became difficult to stop.

If the adventures of Pinaud were so complicated and so exciting—and since certain enlightened people had actually paid his chronicler money to read them this statement not only needs no further confirmation but is not to be lightly dismissed—how much more complicated and more exciting must be the career of M. le Chef, his employer?

M. Pinaud was an individual. M. le Chef controlled the destinies of dozens of detectives. In case any one of them—perhaps a little inflated or a trifle flushed with success—ever dared to forget or ignore that all-important fact, this technique had been specifically evolved to restore assumptions and attitudes to their correct and pre-ordained equilibrium....

'Ah yes, Pinaud,' declared the august personage at last, having finally settled to his own satisfaction the identity of his caller and why he had been summoned. He glanced at the single sheet of notepaper he held in his hand.

'You sent for me, m'sieu,' M. Pinaud put in swiftly, before he had a chance to continue, thereby successfully avoiding committing the unpardonable sin of interrupting M. le Chef when he was actually speaking.

M. Pinaud had a logical mind. It could do no harm to have certain points made quite clear from the very beginning. The first one was obviously that he, Pinaud, was not in the habit of earning his pitiful and inadequate salary by wandering uninvited around the office building, and particularly not along the first floor, at any time of the day. The second, just as obvious, was that—

11

'So I did,' the sharp incisive voice broke in on his meditations. 'And for this reason, Pinaud. Now listen carefully.

'Yesterday the unidentified and weighted body of a man was taken from the river. Some of the weights had not been securely tied, and we surmised that the twin screws of one of these larger express barges had disturbed and driven it from its resting place into the current and the path of a patrolling police-launch.

'The nearest place is called Mitterand, where there is a wharf and a warehouse. We have traced the barge in a hurry. We know exactly when it passed this wharf. We have data on the speed of the current, and the inspector on the launch naturally recorded the time and the precise place when and where they picked up the body.

'The mathematics were complicated and the calculations endless, but we kept at them until we had the answers. It would seem that this wharf and warehouse are well worth investigating. It is almost certain that he was shot and thrown in there.'

M. Pinaud listened attentively, his features expressionless.

'Now you know and I know, Pinaud,' M. le Chef continued at once without giving him the chance to speak even had he wished to, 'that it has become fashionable and customary these days to sneer at, ridicule and denigrate all police-work, but nevertheless in this case we have had some really brilliant deduction in the forensic laboratory concerning the bridge-work in the corpse's teeth. The effects of decomposition—the body must have been in the water at least a week—and the appetite of the local fish cannot have made their task an easy nor a pleasant one.

'From the enquiries and consultations of dental records which followed, we know that the man was named Henri Rostand, aged forty-five, married, and employed as accountant by Roche Enterprises. He had been shot in the back of the head. His wife Yvette reported to the police that he was missing four days ago.'

He laid the sheet of paper down carefully in the exact centre of his blotting-pad and looked up over the rims of his spectacles.

'What are you on now, Pinaud?' he asked.

If I were a Chief of Detectives, M. Pinaud thought swiftly and savagely and bitterly—which I am not, even after so many years of hard and conscientious and unrewarded labour—I would make a point of knowing each day exactly where and what every man on my staff was located and doing—how else could I direct and co-ordinate and cope with the unexpected, and therefore there would be no need to ask such stupid—

Suddenly he realized that M. le Chef was looking at him, waiting for an answer to his question. With a great effort he wrenched his mind back from introspection.

'If you will remember, m'sieu,' he replied quietly, 'I was transferred at a moment's notice, suddenly and unexpectedly, at your special request, from the case of the homosexual salesman to that of the incestuous schoolgirl.'

'Ah yes—of course. I remember.'

'She had intercourse,' M. Pinaud continued rapidly, now warming to his subject, 'not only with her father and grandfather, but also with three of her uncles and one of her brothers. All these gentlemen have now received anonymous letters threatening exposure and hinting at blackmail. I found out when I went to the school to interview her that she is very friendly with a professor of mathematics there. I talked to him as well. He seems to have a great influence over her. My theory was that he may well be the originator and instigator of the whole scheme.

'You gave me to understand, m'sieu, I am sure you will recall, that there had been considerable pressure put on you by the family, who because of their prominent and eminently respectable position in society did not take kindly to the thought of scandal. They are acquaintances of yours, I believe. The father holds an influential position as chairman of—'

'Yes—yes,' interrupted M. le Chef irritably. 'I know all that. But it can't be helped. Have you arrested this professor yet?'

'There is no evidence as to—'

'Rubbish. Rot. Nonsense. Cock. We'll lock him up on some other charge and let him sweat until he confesses. She will get over it. The young are wonderfully resilient. She will probably make a fortune writing her memoirs under another name for one of the more advanced magazines. But this—this is murder, Pinaud. Someone shot Henri Rostand in the back of the head and then weighted his body and dropped it in the river so that it would never be found.'

'I realize that.'

'Well then, he was wrong. He made a mistake. The body has been found. Therefore you must get on with it and find him as soon as possible. We don't like murder here, as you know. Some of the more unpleasant facets of human nature we may have to accept until the owners of such characters transgress the law. Then we can do something. But not murder. With murder we neither wait not accept.'

He paused and glared fiercely over the tops of his spectacles.

Anyone would think that he is interviewing a new recruit, reflected M.

Pinaud sombrely. Why should he assume that I need this kind of pep-talk? He is upset because I have done nothing yet about the schoolgirl, and so he is taking it out on me. Not many—probably not one—of his other detectives would have been able to give him a logical and credible explanation of such a mess. Let him just start his nonsense and then the fat will swiftly and surely be in the fire. He will have a front-page scandal in two days. He ought to know—

He realized that M. le Chef was speaking. Perhaps he had never stopped.

'You go and see Yvette Rostand, Pinaud, right away—even before you go to Mitterand. I telephoned her this morning. She is at home, not well. Normally I believe she works for the same company. Roche Enterprises. Here is the address. She is expecting you.'

There was no need to answer. This was a definite order and the case was now his. He turned towards the door.

M. le Chef's voice, unusually gentle and compassionate, halted him before he reached it.

'I did not tell her, Pinaud. One does

not give such news over the telephone. You do this for me. It will not hurt so much if she is told with sympathy and kindness.'

'Of course, m'sieu.'

'Thank you, Pinaud.'

* * * *

The block of flats was a typical modern building, huge and high and symmetrical, in the fashionable residential quarter of the Sixteenth Arrondissement.

There was a canopied doorway with white flints on either side of the black marble entrance floor and an enormous doorman, in a uniform which called to mind not only an Eastern European field marshal but also a circus bandsman, to superintend that no one kicked the white flints out of place to profane the polished sanctity of his black marble flooring.

Inside, in the awesome hush that only money can buy, there were sunken globes of light, glowing even at that hour, potted palms and wall-to-wall carpeting, rich and luxurious.

18

A receptionist, whose uniform glittered with gold braid of such massive thickness that it seemed doubtful whether he would ever be able to sit down at his switchboard, looked frankly astounded that an individual as ordinary as M. Pinaud had ever been able to pass his colleague in the doorway.

Comprehension and understanding quickly succeeded astonishment and he did everything except actually hold out his hand for another of the expected and gargantuan tips which his colleague in the doorway must obviously have already extracted.

M. Pinaud showed his credentials.

'There is no need to telephone to announce me,' he said politely. 'I have the authority to see Madame Rostand whether she agrees or not. What number and which floor, please?'

The receptionist, although disappointed, did not argue. M. Pinaud's voice was mild and his manner civil, but he was used to having his own way.

'Fourth floor, m'sieu. Number eight. But it is usual to announce a visitor—'

'Then do so if you like. It does not

19

matter.'

There was also a liftman, who looked from his regalia as though he could easily have just relinquished the supreme command of some Arabian potentate's air force because he preferred to press all the complicated buttons of an express lift in order to save himself confrontation with the manifold problems of human relationships.

He too did everything but actually hold out his hand and ask, but M. Pinaud, bearing in mind M. le Chef's choleric reactions to items such as gratuities on expense-sheets, did not relent and therefore did not respond.

Only when the lift had deposited him, soundlessly and efficiently, on the fourth floor, did he begin to wonder.

It was strange, he thought, that a married woman who apparently worked for the same firm as her husband—thereby implying that the extra income was necessary—should be able to afford the luxury of such an apartment.

It was also strange, he reflected as he began to walk along the seemingly endless low-ceilinged corridor towards

Number eight, that this individual now approaching him, walking slowly and almost idly, should also be a tenant and hence able to afford not only the exorbitant rent but also the almost daily toll of those three all but outstretched and avid palms on the lower floor.

He was a small and elderly man with thinning fair hair, faded blue eyes and a lined and tragic face. He wore a respectable but by no means expensive suit and his linen was clean and immaculate.

He gave M. Pinaud a strangely intent look as they passed, almost as if he were trying to memorize this stranger's features, but he did not stop walking and passed towards the far end of the corridor and lift.

* * * *

He had to wait a long time before the door opened.

Then he looked at her with interest, discarding the words he had been about to say. This was not what he had expected.

She had once been beautiful. Until

21

quite recently she must have been lovely. But strain and tension and illness had each drawn veils over that beauty and loveliness until they only looked like ghosts behind the swirling of mists.

He imagined he was looking at the ruins of a cathedral. All the beauty and the fine proportion of her bone-structure were still there—the broad white brow, the high and intelligent cheekbones, the clear and dominant line of jaw—but now, betrayed by the flesh, they were haggard and drawn, and discernible where they should have been implied—as sunlight through the clerestory windows suggests the soaring sweep of rafters to roof, the proportions of fluted pillars and the graceful strength of arches built to sustain such incredible weights—not the bare beams from which plaster has fallen, not a crumbling ruin of stone and the broken sagging of masonry and brick...

This was once a cathedral, he thought, alive with the majesty and grandeur of a work of supreme dedication. But all that made it a cathedral is dead. Here is a body without a soul. Here is a ghost, opening the door to me. Here perhaps is the devil, who moved into the ruin to find a home. I don't know.

Aloud he spoke quietly.

'Madame Rostand?'

'Yes. You must be M'sieu Pinaud. They told me you would call. Please come inside.'

She held the door wide. The words were light and uninflected, quick and easy and gracious—words plucked from a storehouse of memories to be used on an occasion such as this—words which were meaningless and uncaring. Words which could conceal so successfully all the thoughts behind that wide full brow.

'Thank you, madame.'

She was withdrawn and as full of tension as a coiled spring. There were no tears in the brilliant sapphire-blue eyes. They would come later, he thought with pity and compassion, once he had told her. And yet it was strange that she had not asked. One would have thought her very first words would have—

'You have news of my husband, I understand, M'sieu Pinaud?'

'Yes, madame,' he replied quietly.

23

This was not going to be easy.

He looked around the living room into which she had ushered him, trying quickly and almost desperately to marshal his thoughts and decide what to say. It was long and low and luxurious, in keeping with the enormous settee on whose corner he now sat, stiffly upright and unrelaxed—a room furnished regardless of expense by a designer with skill and talent and very good taste—and yet completely lacking every personal and intimate touch that would have made it a home.

'You reported to the police that he was missing, I understand?'

She sat down opposite him and crossed her legs. Her every movement exuded a sexual appeal and magnetism all the more compelling in that it seemed entirely unconscious. In spite of himself his glance flickered downwards.

'Yes, a few days ago. But I have not seen him for over a week. I did not worry at first—he is often away on business.'

'But surely he would let you know—'

'Not always. Sometimes I got a telephone message or a letter after he had gone, if the business was urgent.'

'I see. Business for Roche Enterprises?'

'Yes. I work there too. I am one of Conrad Roche's personal secretaries. But I have been ill—that is why I am at home.'

'I am sorry to hear that,' he said gravely. 'I hope that you will soon be better.'

'Thank you.'

His voice changed again. The polite concern of common courtesy became rich with a genuine sympathy and compassion. 'Madame Rostand,' he said, very gently and very quietly, 'I am afraid it is my duty to bring you some very sad news—'

'About Henri?' she interrupted quickly.

Quickly, factually and mercifully, he gave her the details. Her expression did not change. No tears came to dim the brilliant blue eyes.

'I had—' she began and then stopped suddenly. 'Where?'

'I beg your pardon?'

'Where was he found?'

'By a wharf near the St Denis canal.'

'But where?'

'The place is called Mitterand.'

'That is it—that is the name. One of the Roche companies has a wharf and a warehouse there. I heard Henri mention it several times.'

He thought swiftly and then made his voice impersonal.

'Madame Rostand, we have, from the Bureau of Missing Persons, all the details you gave the police when you reported your husband's disappearance. Would you have any other information of any kind which will help me now in my investigation into his death?'

For a long moment there was silence—a stillness which to his sensitive awareness was fraught with tension and unease and an indefinable feeling of apprehension he could not understand.

Twice she began to speak and twice she hesitated and changed her mind, deciding not to tell him what she had been about to say.

Then finally she came to a decision.

'M'sieu Pinaud, my husband is—was —considerably older, but in spite of the difference in age our marriage was a complete success. We were very happy together.'

She paused for a moment. The blue eyes were looking at him, but he knew they did not see him.

'That is—until recently. Something happened in the last few weeks—I don't know what. Henri would never discuss it. I gather he found out something that Roche was planning to do and would not agree to it. This, mind you, is only a guess on my part. As I said, he refused to discuss it and said that he did not wish to bring his business problems home. But I could see that it worried him. He had several nightmares lately—which he never had before—and woke up shouting and screaming. And sometimes he talked in his sleep.'

'What did he say?'

M. Pinaud was deeply interested.

'Oh—nothing—just nonsense. Once it was something about a river and a barge. And he carried a letter in his pocket-book for weeks, but would never show it to me.'

She paused.

'So really, madame,' he said quietly, 'you have very little to tell me. Just this idea that something was wrong at his business.'

'Yes. I am sorry. But I am quite definitely convinced that I am right.'

'No quarrels? You did not ever try to bring the subject out into the open—to make an issue of it and find out just what was wrong?'

'I told you I tried and that he refused to talk about it. He withdrew into a world of his own which did not include me. Oh—and about a month ago he had to fly to Gothenburg at a moment's notice. Normally he would have taken me with him. I often used to accompany him on these short trips—there was no difficulty in arranging my time off. But on this occasion he did not even ask. I forget the name—some firm of marine engineers.'

'Spanlo?'

She looked at him in surprise.

'Yes. That was it. How did you know?'

'They are famous.'

'I see. I am afraid I don't know very much about that sort of thing.'

28

She looked at her watch and stood up suddenly. M. Pinaud began to get up but she held out her hand to restrain him.

'No—please. I have just remembered I am due for my medicine. I won't be a moment.'

She turned and went out of the room, leaving him alone with his thoughts. They were vivid and chaotic and confused, but he had no time even to begin to sort them out, because in a very short while she was back again, a flush on the high cheekbones, the vivid and lovely eyes even more brilliantly blue than before.

He looked at her carefully and thoughtfully and then stood up for himself.

'I will not take up any more of your time, Madame Rostand,' he said quietly. 'Thank you for your courtesy and patience, and for what you have told me about—'

'It was not very much,' she interrupted.

'No,' he agreed, 'but it may prove of use. If anything else should occur to you later on, please give me a ring. Here is my card. No—no—please don't get up—you

29

are ill. I can easily let myself out.'

He ignored her protests and insisted that she remain seated. Then he thanked her once again very politely and let himself out of the flat, pulling the front door shut quickly behind him.

He wondered which doctor was attending her and whether the drugs she was obviously taking had been prescribed by him as part of his treatment. He wondered if the tears had come by now, to bring her at last an anodyne to her grief. He wondered why she had not cried when she mentioned the business trips they had taken together—if they had been happy in their marriage these were memories which normally would have been almost unbearable in their anguish.

* * * *

He was still wondering when he reached the end of the corridor and the lift. This was why he had not noticed the man waiting there for him. It was the same small and elderly individual who had eyed him so intently as they passed each other before.

Now he pushed the lift button and stepped forward with a determination that was even greater than his pronounced air of deferential apology.

'Excuse me,' he said, 'but I understand that you are M'sieu Pinaud.'

'Yes.'

'From the *Sûreté?*'

'Yes.'

He could have found this out from the individual encased in gold braid at the reception desk. It was no secret. There was no point in denying it.

The man hesitated. The ready answers to his two questions seemed to have destroyed most of his determination.

'Could I speak to you, m'sieu—confidentially—for a few moments?'

'Why—of course.'

Then M. Pinaud too, hesitated.

'May I ask your name, m'sieu?'

'Naturally. I am Victor Marvin.'

M. Pinaud was none the wiser. But at the next words he tensed, suddenly alert.

'I am Yvette Rostand's father.'

M. Pinaud glanced over the man's shoulder. The lift had ascended soundlessly and the doors had opened without any noise. The attendant was fiddling with the bank of buttons on his panel and obviously listening with eager attention.

'In that case,' he said quietly, 'I would suggest, M'sieu Marvin, that you permit me to offer you a glass of wine, over which we shall be sure that our conversation is indeed confidential.'

And then he stepped into the lift. Victor Marvin followed. The attendant punched the buttons viciously, obviously sulking, and shot them down to the ground floor in a few seconds.

If he held out his hand, no one saw it. Both his passengers were outside almost as soon as the lift stopped.

'I noticed a *café* somewhere here as I came,' M. Pinaud said, leading the way along the main boulevard.

Soon they were seated at an end table under the gaily-striped awning in complete privacy.

M. Pinaud, without any qualms at all, ordered a large carafe of Anjou. He knew exactly what effect any figures in the entertainment column of his expense-sheet had upon M. le Chef's blood-pressure, but he also knew that an open Anjou was a lovely if somewhat treacherous wine, and that therefore whatever the father of Yvette Rostand had to tell him would be told more eloquently if perhaps less explicitly, more fully if perhaps a little less coherently and certainly more completely and confidentially possibly even than the narrator knew.

He raised his glass, which the waiter had filled. The wine was exquisitely chilled. If necessary he would pay for the carafe himself.

'Your good health, M'sieu Marvin,' he said gravely. 'What is it you have to tell me?'

'Thank you. And yours.'

Marvin drank deeply and gave a great sigh of satisfaction.

'You must forgive me for accosting you in this manner, M'sieu Pinaud, but I am nearly out of my mind with worry—'

He paused as M. Pinaud refilled his glass.

'Don't stop,' he said quietly and sympathetically as he put the carafe down. 'About Yvette?'

'Yes. She is ill.'

'I know.'

'Far more ill than she will admit.'

He drank again and then leaned forward across the table.

'Let me tell you all about it. She is my only daughter. We were always good friends—great friends. Her mother died when she was quite young. It did not seem to make much difference at the time—she was still her daddy's girl as she always has been—but I see now how that was the beginning of the end. A young girl needs a mother—she is the only one necessary—she is the one who can help and comfort and advise. A father is not the right person. Somehow I failed her— I can't think how or why. We drifted apart very quickly as she grew up, with a will and a spirit and a determination of her own. She went her own way—moved out—and left me to go mine. We visited each other occasionally, but we—who had once been so close—were two strangers making commonplace remarks in a meaningless conversation. We had drifted in opposite directions for so many years—now we no longer knew each other.'

He paused, sighed dejectedly and eyed his empty glass wistfully. M. Pinaud immediately refilled it.

'You must not let that worry you, M'sieu Marvin,' he said kindly. 'It happens to the majority of parents.'

Yvette's father drank again.

'Yes,' he continued. 'From what my friends have told me and from my own observations, I would say that you are right. One should be practical.'

He sighed again and eyed his glass in malignant reproach, as if blaming it for being nearly empty.

M. Pinaud sighed too, for a different reason, swiftly refilled the glass and held up the empty carafe, just in time to catch the eye of a waiter who was passing their table.

Marvin cheered up a little at the sight of his brimming glass.

'How can I be practical?' he went on. 'I am an idealist, a romantic and a per-fectionist. As well tell me to grow two more feet.'

He paused long enough to half-empty his glass in one gigantic swallow.

'I was so happy when she told me that

she was going to marry Henri Rostand. Of course I was also bitterly disappointed as well—what parent ever thinks any bride or groom is worthy of his magnificent children—but I did not say anything. I met him. Then I began to feel glad and happy. Then I knew that she was fortunate. He was older, but that did not matter. He was a fine type with a brilliant intellect. He had a good position with Roche and a great future in such a vast organization.'

Again he paused, leaned a little closer to M. Pinaud and then spoke with a great intensity.

'But above all he was kind. Kind and considerate. To me that was the most important thing of all. How many people today, M'sieu Pinaud, are like false and glittering shells—presenting an outward show of charm and good humour and conviviality—while underneath and inside they are sick and warped and twisted and cruel?'

'Too many,' agreed M. Pinaud gravely. He refilled their glasses and lit a cigarette. This could be the Anjou talking now and no longer Victor Marvin. He offered the packet but the other man shook his head.

'They were happy at first. I knew they would be. They invited me to their apartment many times, and after all the sad and wasted years of drifting I felt that I had found my daughter again.'

His voice died and the faded blue eyes grew dim as he sought to escape into his own dream world of memory. Then he roused himself with a great effort, reached out for his glass and drank again, hurriedly, fiercely, desperately.

'Then, recently,' he continued, 'something went wrong. I don't know what. Yvette would not tell me and will not tell me now. I tried to talk to her. I offered to help. I argued. I pleaded. I even threatened. It was all of no use. Her manner became so strange—I could no longer understand her. We quarrelled—violently and bitterly. She told me not to come here any more—to stop interfering —to leave her alone—she told me this— me, her own father.'

He lifted his glass and drank again.

'Now she refuses to see me—shuts the door in my face. I have to hang about outside this building, watching everyone who comes in. I have retired from business and therefore have plenty of time. Then I follow them inside and walk about up and down the corridor, trying to make sure that she is all right and not—'

'Why shouldn't she be?' interrupted M. Pinaud quietly.

Marvin stared at him sadly.

'I don't know,' he replied, slowly and hopelessly. 'So many small things are not right. She no longer seems like my daughter. She looks at me as if I were a stranger. It is as if someone else were using her mind and body. When she was young she used to come to me for advice and help—then I felt it was all worth while, whatever the trouble, whatever the problem. Now I am an interfering old busybody. And a pompous old fool. She no longer has time for me.'

He sighed once more and closed his eyes for a moment as he paused.

'I know I am sentimental—I have always been. I still keep the sampler she embroidered when she was at her convent school and the black shoes she wore for her confirmation. Why, you will ask—why? It does no good. What is the use of looking backwards?

'But when one grows old, M'sieu Pinaud—and suddenly some day sees children who are no longer children but grown-up strangers—then one is forced to look back and try to live on memories, since there is no point in looking forward any more. The time is too short.'

He raised his glass and drank deeply again.

'When you yourself grow old, M'sieu Pinaud, you will find out that most of your desires will vanish—except two.'

'And what are those?'

'The first one is a desire for peace. Most of us spend our whole lives rushing about and worrying and striving to achieve something—always praying, always hoping, always believing that when we finally succeed it will all have been worth the effort. Nothing could be more false. All we find out—when it is too late —is that we have never had time to know that peace which gives the whole point and meaning to life. The second is that those we love may know that peace and happiness before it is too late.'

M. Pinaud poured out carefully into their glasses what wine was left in the second carafe. For a moment he debated with himself as to whether he should order another one, and then firmly rejected the idea.

After all, this confidential talk had told him nothing more then he already knew. He was wasting not only his time but probably his own money as well, since it was highly improbable that M. le Chef would authorize any item listed on his expense-sheet as entertainment of the deceased's father-in-law. If only he could have added to the sub-column to entertainment entitled Reasons and Explanations something like this: In Order to Obtain Valuable and Vital Information Essential to the Apprehension of the Murderer—then he might have had a chance.

Now he had none, because his conscience would never allow him to write such nonsense.

He was lighting another cigarette when Marvin spoke again.

'Your kindness, your courtesy and

your magnificent hospitality, M'sieu Pinaud,' he said, 'give me the courage to ask you a question. I do not know if it is ethical. Please tell me if I presume.'

'What is it?'

'I found out that Yvette reported Henri as missing a few days ago. Now you, from the *Sûreté,* are calling to see her. Does that mean—'

'Yes,' M. Pinaud interrupted, quietly and slowly and with gentle sympathy. 'I am sorry. It means that he is dead and his body has been found and identified. He was shot in the back of the head and the body was weighted and dropped into the river. It means also that I am investigating the murder. Otherwise an official from the Bureau of Missing Persons would have taken my place.'

For a long moment there was silence.

'I too am sorry,' said Marvin at length. 'He was a good man.'

He sighed deeply.

'That is what we always say about the dead—but it does not bring them back. Have you any clues?'

M. Pinaud smiled.

'That is a question I do not answer.'

'Of course—forgive me—'

He stood up, not without difficulty and somewhat unsteadily. Anjou is a treacherous wine.

'I am glad that you are investigating the case, M'sieu Pinaud. Everyone has heard of you. And I am sure it will help Yvette. I know she will feel better when once you have caught Henri's murderer. She has had a worrying time lately, with all the anxiety of his disappearance and now the shock of the news you have just brought her—'

M. Pinaud stood up as well and interrupted him quietly.

'Yes.'

If she had cried, he thought—if only she could have found tears for a dead husband—then he might have believed him.

'I am sure she will feel better once all this has been settled. Now I must go. If I were you, M'sieu Marvin I would sit down and order a pot of strong black coffee. This is a very strong wine.'

He said good-bye and left, hoping that his good advice would not be ignored.

CHAPTER 2

It was a typical river warehouse, functional and practical, designed and built for one purpose. It fronted the two mobile cranes on the quay, alongside which was moored a modern barge with a large wheelhouse, riding high in the water. The cobbled by-road made a loop, rising on a slight incline to the level of the bollards and then descending the other side to rejoin the main road.

M. Pinaud stopped his car before the rise, left his engine running quietly and looked at everything very carefully.

The vast sliding doors of the warehouse were wide open and a heavy lorry had been backed half-way into the building with its radiator facing the road. In spite of the presence of the lorry, the place seemed deserted. There was no sound and no movement.

He accelerated, let in the clutch and drove his car up the slope, parking it diagonally across the front of the lorry.

As he got out on the far side two shots cracked in rapid succession and he felt the wind of their passage ruffle his hair.

He dropped flat to take cover behind his car. When he rose to his knees his gun was in his hand. He turned and crawled cautiously towards the back of the car and then, lying almost prone, looked under the overhang of the rear fender.

He could not see anyone, only the front section of the empty floor of the warehouse. There was no movement. There was no target.

With his free hand he felt in his side pocket.

Now here, for the benefit of those who are both curious and meticulous, his chronicler (who is concerned only with the truth) hastens to add that the army grenade M. Pinaud extracted from his pocket was not and never had been part of the orthodox armament of detectives in the *Sûreté,* but he was fortunate in having as a friend the colonel at St Cyr who was chief instructor in weapon training to the young and hopeful cadets who one day—if they could endure his caustic tongue for so long—would provide the flower of the officer-class in the French Army.

It was the standard Mark II type with a three-second fuse. As he laid his gun down carefully and gently on a large and clean cobblestone, released the clip and clasped the plunger tightly, encircling the whole grenade with his hand, he reflected thankfully—in case M. le Chef felt like asking awkward questions afterwards—that it was just as well that the colonel had signed for it and not him.

Just now, in this situation, it was the ideal weapon. There was not much point in firing his gun at nothing.

He rose slowly to his hands and knees and tensed his muscles. Then suddenly, in one fluid movement, he sprang up and hurled the grenade over the tope of his car and into the open doorway.

Another two shots splintered the rear window as he dropped down again under cover and a second later the roar of the explosion engulfed and obliterated the mad chatter of a burst of automatic fire he felt thudding into and ricocheting off the bodywork of his car.

His aim had been good, but in the excitement of trying to keep his exposure to a minimum he must have thrown too hard and too far. The noise was still resounding in his head when two men suddenly dashed out from the side of the building and jumped into the cab of the lorry from the far side. One carried a Sten gun and one a revolver.

The door banged, the engine roared into life and the lorry was already moving by the time M. Pinaud ran round the back of his car. He only had time for two quick snapshots at the lorry's windscreen and then was forced to leap back again the way he had come, to crouch and regain the cover of his car.

Only this time he did not get too close. He knew what was going to happen to his car, which he had parked there deliberately to block the lorry's exit. At the time he had thought, mistakenly and yet understandably, that this expedition to Mitterand would probably involve a routine search and some questions, if necessary at the point of a gun—and not an ambush and a miniature battle.

He was right about the fate of his car.

With a sickening crunch of mangled metal the massive iron fender of the lorry crashed into the side of his car and flung it out of the way as if it had been a child's toy. M. Pinaud jumped farther back only just in time.

But he did not anticipate the effect of the two quick shots he had fired. The windscreen of the lorry was an opaque sheet of splintered glass. The driver had his head stuck out of the far window in an effort to see where he was going. This was satisfactory as far as it went, but not being a contortionist and being incapable, like most human beings, of elongating his neck, he could not see the low iron bollard directly in the path of his right front wheel as he accelerated violently away after the crashing impact with the stationery car.

His tyre hit the bollard with a force that nearly tore the steering wheel from his hand. The lorry, out of control, swerved dangerously near one of the mobile cranes. In his anxiety to avoid the massive iron wheels and rails the driver must had over-corrected his swerve and perhaps underestimated the gathering momentum of his powerfully accelerating back wheels—no one would ever know.

The lorry swerved not to the right—too far—and then the front wheel dipped over the edge of the quay. The back tyres screamed as the driver jammed on the brakes, but the cobbles were old and worn and greasy, and the momentum of his violent and thrusting acceleration was too great.

The locked tyres slid inexorably forward. The other front wheel and the radiator dropped. With dreadful and horrifying slowness the lorry slid forward on its chassis girders, tilted even more, and then plunged forward and downward into the river, just beside the stern of the barge.

M. Pinaud, gun in hand, had been ready to run from the moment his car had been hit. He wondered why the two men had not wrenched open the doors and jumped to safety. There had been ample time.

Then he remembered the crashing impact of the lorry into his own car and his run slowed to a walk. That could easily have jammed both doors of the cab. In that case there was no need to run.

He came to the side of the quay, holstered his gun and leaned over, looking down at the water.

There was nothing to be seen, nothing to be done. If the doors had been free, they would have torn them open and jumped. Obviously they had jammed. The splintered and shattered windscreen would not keep the water out for long. By the time he could collect any underwater rescue equipment they would be dead.

Suddenly he shivered, as if with cold. They had tried to murder him, for no other reason than that he was trying to do his duty. Someone had paid them money to kill him. He felt no remorse.

And yet—and yet—two human beings —two men who had been alive a few moments before were now dead—horribly and agonizingly dead. He felt no regret, although in the execution of his duty he himself had definitely been the cause of their death.

And yet he felt compassion, for that

was his nature. He crossed himself and prayed for their souls.

＊＊＊＊

Then he went inside the warehouse, his gun ready in his hand.

The building still reeked of cordite and amytol, although the large jagged section which had been blown out of the back wall admitted enough air to make a draught through the open sliding doors. There were bales and sacks and boxes everywhere, stacked up against the walls. The centre of the floor was bare.

The two men must have been crouching just inside the far sliding doors, protected from the blast of the grenade by a pile of sacks which had probably been stacked high at the time of the explosion. Now the centre ones had disintegrated and the pile was an untidy heap, lying on a mound of white granules.

He bent down, scooped up a little and tasted. It was sugar. Most of the stacks of boxes had labels or stencilled lettering to confirm his taste. He walked around the building slowly, examining everything carefully, and then holstered his gun. There did not seem to be any evidence that this was anything else but a sugar warehouse.

Which made it all the more strange that he should have been ambushed and nearly killed the moment he approached it. Had there been something to hide, something illegal, it would have been easier to understand.

He spent more time there, walking around and examining everything conscientiously, but without success. Then he went outside and looked again at the barge, confirming that it was obviously unladen.

Wondering, he went back to his car.

Apparently there was nothing wrong, nothing illegal or out of order, no proof or evidence that would justify any action being taken. And yet here, or near here, the accountant Henri Rostand had been shot in the back of the head, his body weighted and flung into the river, leaving a widow who could find no tears to mourn her husband's murder.

For a moment he had the frustrating and yet not altogether unfamiliar feeling that this was a case about which he understood very little....

He shrugged philosophically. This was not the first time he had felt the same at the beginning of a case and in all probability it would not be the last. And yet in the end he solved them all. Some took longer and some were a little harder, that was all. Tomorrow was another day. Tomorrow something would happen and that would tell him which way to turn, which lead to follow. It had happened before. It would happen again.

His car was badly damaged. The repairs would obviously take some considerable time.

Gloomily, as he contemplated its shattered side, he thought of M. le Chef and of the effect any accident always had on his blood-pressure. He remembered the countless claim-forms he had methodically, conscientiously and laboriously filled in during the course of his adventurous career, and how M. le Chef had personally supervised and checked the drawing of each of the required sketch-maps depicting the position of his vehicle at the time of the accident.

Anyone would be entitled to think that the old bastard owned the insurance company (which he might well have done) and that it was his own money at stake. It could be that it was.

For a moment he considered using the radio-telephone to contact the office—if it was still working—and waiting here patiently until M. le Chef himself could drive out here to see the evidence with his own eyes. That would at least save a lot of the usual argument as to whether the accident had been in any way due to his own carelessness, recklessness, negligence or—bearing in mind that the car was somewhat overdue for replacement —sheer bloody-mindedness.

And then he suddenly remembered what day it was.

There was no time to wait for M. le Chef, who was quite capable of delaying his departure, of taking the most circuitous and involved route and driving along it deliberately at a snail's pace—if only to express his disapproval of subordinates (even the most privileged and the most celebrated) who smashed up expensive cars on routine assignments.

There was no time to put up with all that nonsense. This was a special day. This was the day on which Germaine, his beloved wife, had decided to visit one of her numerous cousins in the country for a week. All the arrangements had been made and the children already parked with her parents at Passy.

Her train was due to leave the Gare St Lazare at five-forty-five. He had planned to take her and her luggage to the station in his car as soon as he finished work. To count on being able to find a taxi at that time, in the height of the rush-hour, was not only optimistic but foolish.

Now he would have to telephone for a hired car, since the luggage Germaine considered essential for a week's visit precluded any other form of transport.

When he had ventured to point out mildly and tentatively—since in his profession it was tempting Providence to make appointments at such a time—that on the numerous occasions on which he had to go away himself he never took more than one small case with shirts, pyjamas and underclothes, she looked at him with that all-too-familiar expression

54

of loving and yet slightly exasperated affection mingled with a great and genuine amazement.

'But—at this time of the year one can never tell whether it is going to be hot or cold. One must take suitable clothes for both eventualities, in order to be prepared. And you ought to know by now—however light you may travel yourself—that for a woman such a thing is an impossibility. For a woman it is essential to have shoes to match the different colours of suits and dresses. Besides, in that house there are never enough coat-hangers or shoe-trees—these things must therefore be packed as well. I know this all makes extra weight, and I am sorry to give you all this trouble. You are the one who has to carry the cases down the stairs. And then I have to take all those presents for the children—young Philippe's building-bricks must be made of concrete. They are so heavy it would cost a fortune to send them by post. And they would probably break the box and then his present would never even get delivered—'

And so on and so forth. He listened

patiently, with tolerance, love and under-standing. After all, it was an indisputable fact that *le bon Dieu* had created women in a different mould, even the best, and a wise man accepted this fact with a philo-sophical resignation.

He had decided to stop work and leave for home in good time, whatever the cir-cumstances. His wife, in his opinion, was considerably more important to him than his cases, even if that of M. le Chef might differ.

He sighed as he tried to open the apparently undamaged doors on the other side of his car. Life had a habit of suddenly becoming very complicated all at once. But at least he ought to tell them at the office what had happened.

Both doors were jammed. The shock of the impact must have been strong enough to warp and distort the whole body-shell. He tried his keys, without much hope, and without success. Even if his radio-telephone were undamaged, he could not use it.

He gave up and looked inside the warehouse. The telephone had once been against the far wall. Now a few strands of blackened wire and fragments of shattered vulcanite on the floor added their mute and entirely unnecessary testimonial to the efficiency of the colonel's grenade.

Moodily, he went outside, lit a cigarette and began to walk towards the nearest building in search of a telephone.

* * * *

Now it was evening, and he was alone.

Now all the tumult and the shouting had died. Now the bugle had blown peace.

The tumult had been engendered by the carting of Germaine's three suitcases down the narrow flights of stairs to the hired car, with the *concièrge* capering about like an infuriated she-monkey, always two steps behind him, gibbering with agonized fear lest one of their corners should chip a flake from her precious and immaculate paint.

The shouting had been by M. le Chef, whose rage and indignation at the damage to M. Pinaud's car—coupled with the frustration of realizing that it would be his own department's responsibility and expense to organize and pay for the salvaging of a heavy lorry containing two corpses which some fearsome and omnipotent organization such as the *Société Générale des Fleuves Intérieures* would insist on being done immediately —caused him to reach a falsetto C note high enough to instil a brief wonder as to whether in his frenzy he might have inadvertently self-inflicted a vital injury....

The peace came from within. It had been a hard and exhausting day. He had honestly tried—as was his habit—to do his best. He had narrowly escaped death. Now at last he was alone.

And although no one could ever deny that he loved his wife dearly, with an intensity of feeling very few men achieved, to an introvert of his character there was always something to be said for being occasionally alone, and thus to have the opportunity of being free to think and to brood and to remember, of being able to surrender completely to one's imagination and watch entranced the images it could so effortlessly create, of not having to talk and to listen and then to talk again....

He lit another cigarette and went into the kitchen. His jacket and shoulder-holster were hanging from the hook behind the kitchen door. He was in his shirt-sleeves and comfortable.

He sat down at the table and poured himself a generous absinthe, allowing the ice-cold water to drain slowly over the cubes of sugar on the strainer, to turn the amber liquid into milky opaqueness.

The day's work was done. Now he could relax. He had not achieved much, apart from saving his own life at the expense of two others and learning very little of use or information from Yvette Rostand and her father.

At least he had tried and done his best. No man could do more. To work hard, to profit by experience and to try again and keep on trying again, as many times as was necessary, until the task was achieved—the rules were simple. They only had to be obeyed.

This had all the appearances and indications of an interesting case. Tomorrow he would go and see Conrad Roche and talk to him about his employees and

59

his warehouse.

At the moment he was both tired and hungry. And he also had a noble thirst.

He finished his drink slowly, enjoying every swallow. Then he poured another. For a while he sat drinking and meditating, relaxing and enjoying himself.

After all the strain and the tensions of the day, his only obligations—it was a pleasing thought—were simple ones. He had to decide how many times he would refill his glass. Absinthe was a wonderful drink after a day's hard work, but it had a treacherous and unpleasant habit later of letting one down—considerably lower than its uplift. He had to taste the stew. He had to get a bottle of wine from the cupboard. And he should cut some bread. He felt supremely confident that he could cope with them all.

He got up, went to the stove and lit the gas beneath the giant saucepan that stood there.

In spite of the complexity of her packing, Germaine had found time to prepare his favourite meal. On this he would live quite happily throughout the week she was away, with such additions and embellishments as his fancy dictated, and therefore she considered it worth while to make the effort.

In this enormous saucepan she had boiled, very slowly and for a long time, a large leg of lamb. In the same water and at the same time she had prepared and added onions, carrots, leeks, turnips, swedes and parsnips. The saucepan was full to the brim. The potatoes were in a smaller and separate saucepan.

After the first meal, he could add what was left of them to the stew, which would save him the trouble of peeling, washing and cooking more. When he had finished the potatoes he could add spaghetti, macaroni or tagliatelle. His meal therefore would always be ready for him at whatever time he came home. His household tasks would be confined to lighting the gas and washing-up. And if he should be very tired, exhausted and discouraged after a particularly difficult or dangerous day—why, then—he could leave all the washing-up—there were enough plates and glasses—until she came home. Thus Germaine.

In later years fate decreed that M.

Pinaud was to pay grievously, not only for his voracious and gargantuan appetite but also for the uncontrolled and unrestrained enthusiasm with which he indulged it on every possible occasion.

One need not be a dietician or a doctor to imagine what effect a week's consumption of the contents of that saucepan would have on his already overstrained and much abused digestive tract.

Mercifully, this he did not know. The mercy of life is that one does not know what is going to happen. It was just as well, otherwise the knowledge might have spoiled his appetite.

Just at that time he was hungry, not quite so thirsty—as he poured out very carefully his fifth glass of absinthe and—for brief, unforgettable and wonderful moments—he was completely happy.

He got up again, took a spoon from the drawer and lifted the lid of the gigantic saucepan. The aroma was so delicious that it seemed to intoxicate him.

He stirred carefully and tasted. Germaine knew exactly how he liked his spices. Exquisite. Perhaps a little—just a little more garlic. He tasted again. And

Cayenne pepper. That would already be on the table, which Germaine had laid in the dining room before she left. He could add that on his plate.

The stew was beginning to bubble. He lifted the lid of the other saucepan. The potatoes in their water were still quite cold. Feeling slightly ashamed, he hastily turned off one gas tap and lit the other one.

Only an idiot, Pinaud, he told himself sternly, would forget to cook potatoes which he has not even had to peel. Now you will have to wait another twenty minutes before you can do justice to this superlative meal. You will obviously have to occupy yourself somehow during all that time—therefore you had better uncork the wine, cut some bread, heat your plate and maybe drink a little more of this excellent absinthe, which should all help you to forget the pangs of this excruciating hunger.

Later, finally, he sat down at the table in the dining room.

All his tasks had been successfully completed. His plate was as hot as its contents, his first glass of wine had been poured, the bread cut and the Cayenne pepper liberally sprinkled.

He remembered, when his plate was half-empty, that he had not eaten any lunch that day. There had been no time.

Then, suddenly, the doorbell rang, loudly, stridently and imperiously.

CHAPTER 3

The man standing outside was tall and powerfully built, extraordinarily handsome in a fleshy and sensual way. His features reminded M. Pinaud strangely of something or someone but he could not for the moment recall what or who. He wore a very expensive suit, with neither overcoat nor hat.

'M'sieu Pinaud?'

His voice was resonant and cultivated, his manner partaking of a passive immobility born of a consciousness of power. He did not have to assert himself. There was no need. Every gesture, every intonation of his voice, was that of a man accustomed to immediate and unquestioning obedience.

'Yes.'

M. Pinaud's voice was calm and quiet, and yet instinctively he tensed, involuntarily he reacted. The man's assured and infuriating assumption of authority immediately made him an antagonist.

'You know who I am?'

'Yes. Conrad Roche. I have seen your photographs.'

'Good. May I come in?'

'Of course.'

M. Pinaud stood aside and ushered him into the dining-room.

'Please sit down.'

'Thank you.'

'Allow me to apologize for the table. I was eating.'

Roche waved a hand with exquisitely manicured finger-nails.

'Then it is I who should be apologizing for interrupting you—'

'Not at all. There is no hurry.'

He pulled out another chair from the table and sat down opposite his visitor.

'I had intended coming myself to see you tomorrow, M'sieu Roche,' he went on, without the slightest change in the inflection of his voice.

'Indeed? And why?'

M. Pinaud sat perfectly still as he replied and yet the tension within him was like that of a coiled spring.

'There is a wharf and a warehouse on

the river, at Mitterand, which belong to one of your companies. I saw Yvette Rostand today. Her husband's body came out of the water by chance there sooner than his murderers expected. We know by now quite a lot about him. He worked for you until he disappeared last week.'

Roche remained imperturbable.

'So? We are meeting earlier, that is all. Your information is quite correct.'

Then he looked pointedly over M. Pinaud's shoulder at the laid table and the plate of congealing stew.

'Eating alone tonight, M'sieu Pinaud?' he continued quietly.

There was no threat, no inflection at all in his voice, and yet suddenly M. Pinaud felt, almost physically, the first clutch of cold fear in his heart and stomach.

He controlled his voice with a great effort.

'I fail to see how it is any concern of yours, M'sieu Roche, but my wife is away visiting her cousins in the country.'

Roche shook his head. The tension between them grew almost palpably.

'No,' he said flatly.

'What do you mean—no?'

'I mean that the driver of the car you hired took her this evening, not to St Lazare, but to a rendezvous where she was persuaded to change into one of mine. She is now in a very safe place.'

There was a long silence.

Suddenly, pungently, the small room was filled with the smell of burning stew.

M. Pinaud sprang to his feet and tore open the door to the kitchen.

'Excuse me—my dinner,' he called over his shoulder as he went.

* * * *

As he turned off the gas the doorbell rang again, and then he heard a thunderous knocking as well.

He went to open the front door. It was Madame Wagner, the occupant of the flat above. She was a vast mountain of a woman, tall and stout and fleshy and she loved the sound of her own voice.

'Well now, M'sieu Pinaud—I am sure you will forgive the liberty but I felt I ought to come down and tell you in case

68

you did not know—although how any-body could not be aware of it is beyond me—but as it is a fairly warm night we had the windows open wide and so we could not help smelling it—'

'I know—I am sorry—'

But no words of his could stem the torrent of hers. Her pause was not to listen to him, but only to regain her breath.

'A most unpleasant—'

He felt that he should not give up try-ing.

'Obviously—it is—'

'Obnoxious would be a good word—'

'Of course, but—'

'Or revolting—'

'Granted—and yet—'

'Even disgusting—'

'Let me explain—'

'Vile and certainly unhealthy—'

'I quite agree but—'

He did not have a chance. She simply would not allow him to speak. And her interruptions were deliberately short and concise, which gave her both the time and the opportunity to draw even more breath into her enormous lungs for another onslaught.

'Now you know and I know, M'sieu Pinaud, that there are on this earth smells and other smells and different smells—and of all the smells that of burnt food is one of the worst—although the normal cooking of cabbage is bad enough—but of course your dear wife is exceptional and I have never had any cause for complaint before but the people below you as you probably know are something different—the times I have had to go down two flights of stairs and of course all the way up again—those boys of hers making sulphuretted hydrogen in their chemistry laboratory at school and smuggling it home to let off on the staircase and smoking their father's cigars and stuffing the lighted butts down the armchairs when they got caught and the smell of corruption and white maggots from her dustbin when the dustmen went on strike in the summer—'

'Look, Madame Wagner, I am very sorry about this—but at the moment I am—'

'Oh I knew you would not mind if I

came down in case you had not realized
—I told my husband and he said you
might get upset but I said not you—after
all we are old neighbours and old friends
and I always feel that when it is a question of a particular smell and a localized
one then it becomes a duty to do something about it because there are so many
smells one has to endure in silence like
the stink-bombs they let off in the Gaul-
list riots and the students' revolt and that
dreadful time when all the main drains
got blocked up—'

This could go on forever. He began,
slowly but definitely, to close the door.

'Madame Wagner, I am very sorry you
have had to come down and I appreciate
your concern. The gas is turned off now
and I am sure the smell will not last. And
now please—you will really have to
excuse me. I have a guest waiting for me
inside—'

'I know that—aha I know—because I
heard the doorbell ring—one can perhaps begin to understand now how the
dinner came to get burnt—'

And she leered at him archly with a
dreadful and triumphant air of lustful

complicity. Then the black and beady eyes contemplated him shrewdly and speculatively, even perhaps a little contemptuously.

'Your wife is away, is she not, M'sieu Pinaud?' she asked him, with a wealth of innuendo in her voice.

He ignored it. He forced himself to keep calm, to answer her quietly without hitting her and to master the sudden and agonizing tension her words forced up inside him as he remembered.

'Yes. She is staying with her cousins. And now, if you will excuse me, Madame Wagner, I will say good night. Thank you once again for coming down.'

* * * *

When he returned to the dining room, having finally got rid of her, his gun was in his hand.

Roche ignored it.

'Allow me to explain the situation,' he said evenly, as if there had been no interruption. 'I have taken some considerable trouble to find out a good deal about you, M'sieu Pinaud. As a result, I have been forced to the conclusion that this is the only way to get what I want.'

'And what is that?'

Roche suddenly stood up in one lithe movement, a dominant and commanding figure. The gun moved slightly, covering his every action, but for all the notice he took it might not have been there.

'I want you to stop interfering with what does not concern you. I want you to stop investigating my affairs, which are my business and not yours.'

M. Pinaud did not answer.

'Some men—most men—have their price. The driver of your hired car is a typical example. Not you. I know that. But you love your wife. This I do know. I need time—a week at least—to finish what I am doing. She will be well treated —provided you do what you are told.'

M. Pinaud shook his head. But still he did not answer.

'You will have to. You will obey my orders to our mutual advantage. There is no point in our harming or hurting her— which would only upset you and drive you to greater efforts to interfere.'

He paused again. Still M. Pinaud did not speak. Then Roche pointed to the gun and the resonant voice changed.

'Let me tell you something, M'sieu Pinaud, and be quite sure that you understand it. If I do not return alone and unharmed, various small but interesting portions of your wife's body will be removed—with or without her consent—with or without an anaesthetic —and delivered here to you personally, one at a time, in a parcel.'

Once more he paused for a moment.

'I can see by your expression that you find this hard to believe. I can assure you that I mean every word and that I shall have no difficulty in having this done. I have a surgeon friend who rather specializes in that sort of thing.'

For a long time there was silence after he had ceased to speak. A silence horrible in its implications, terrifying in the ruthless certainty of its threat.

The gun lowered as M. Pinaud let his arm fall helplessly to his side. His eyes looked everywhere except at Roche. Was it possible that this was the room in which he and his wife had lived together for so many years, the room that had echoed to the tears and laughter of children, the room that once had reflected the hours of love and peace and contentment a family had spent together—the room which once—until now—had been his home?

He shivered as his febrile imagination flashed horrifying images through his mind, and turning slowly, all at once like an old man, he laid his gun down on the sideboard. The blued steel clicked loudly on the polished mahogany.

What could he do? This man held all the cards. Force and a gun were not the answers now. What should he do? Play for time? Try to find out—

Roche interrupted him as if he had been reading his thoughts.

'There is nothing you can do, M'sieu Pinaud. I have laid my plans too well. My friends will be watching you all the time, and I shall know exactly what you are doing. You will not recognize them. You do not even know who they are. But from now on they will be near you and with you and all around you, watching you and reporting to me, day and night, so that I shall always know what you do and where you go.

'Good night, M'sieu Pinaud.'

The front door closed quietly and he was alone.

* * * *

He tried to pray, but he could find no words.

Prayer was a supplication, a humility, even an abasement in accepting an infinite—of whatever creed or conception —as greater than the individual. Prayers he had always said for her, each and every night, since the day they had met.

But now he had no words. Now he felt hard and cold and furious. And resentful that this unfair thing should have happened to him.

He went to stand in the kitchen. For a moment he contemplated the saucepan on the stove. Now he had lost his appetite. He could not bear to think of food.

Then he opened a window. He must have forced the mead down too far, too low against the bottom when he had carved his portion, and then—for some reason he could not understand—left the gas-flame too high while he was eating.

Why not take the meat out and carve it on a dish, he asked himself. Because it might have got cold. As you intended re-filling your plate five or six times you thought it should have been kept hot. There is an oven. You could have used that. Now you will have to clean the saucepan. There is none other in the place as big. You will then have to trans-fer the stew into two or three smaller ones.

Suddenly he turned, pulled out a chair blindly and sat down. Then he covered his face with his hands and tasted his own tears salt upon his lips.

He felt overwhelmed, crushed and de-feated. And very close to despair.

And yet he could not stop or control his thoughts. They filled his mind in a whirl of confusion, chaotic and relent-less. What manner of man are you, Pinaud, he asked himself with contempt and sadness and bitterness—worrying about a burnt saucepan when your wife has been kidnapped by a madman and is in danger of torture and mutilation and possibly death—she who has never willingly harmed anyone in her life?

This is your nature. When something has to be done you can know no peace until you have done it. And you were brought up as a child on the precept that if a thing is worth doing, then it is worth doing well. Anyone knows that the longer a burnt saucepan is left the harder it is to clean.

Then, Pinaud, it is time for you to forget your precept and if necessary even to deny your nature, so that you can find your wife and kill the man responsible—where is your sense of proportion?

And now, treading with delicate and dream-sandalled feet down the corridors of time, the memories came thronging behind the thoughts, their touch light and compassionate, their tenderness an anguish he could hardly bear.

He remembered her at her parents' dinner-table, to which he had been summoned for inspection at the time of their engagement, telling her father with a passionate and lovable sincerity that there was nothing dishonourable in chasing and capturing criminals.

He remembered her standing beside him in front of the altar, and the love and the pride in her eyes as she turned from the priest to look at him.

He remembered the days and the years of joy and happiness they had shared together, the anxiety and the pain and the sorrow that had fused and tempered their great love into a sacrament time could never destroy.

And then those memories fled grieving as he remembered all the times he had been unkind and impatient and intolerant—all the times when the anxiety and the strain and tension of his profession had driven him thoughtlessly and heedlessly to hurt her—the times when his ambition and his obsession with the advancement of his career had made him forget that her every action, thought and impulse sprang only from her incomparable love for him and her desire to help and please him....

He sat there alone, suffering agonies of remorse at his thoughtlessness, for this again was his nature and it could not be changed.

And then, as inevitably as the cool of

the evening follows the heat of the day, as surely as the dawn breaks after the night, he remembered—with a vividness that was like a cool and comforting hand —her forgiveness, always so graciously and generously given from a nature whose essential goodness and kindness, tenderness and compassion, he still found hard to believe....

The very intensity of his suffering made it an emotion that could not endure. The flames of his sorrow seemed to leap so savagely through his heart and mind and body that soon only the ashes of emptiness remained.

* * * *

He removed his hands.

In front of him, on the table where he had left them in his eagerness to assuage his gargantuan appetite, were the bottle of absinthe, the jug of iced water, the strainer and the bowl of sugar. And his empty glass.

This was not the answer, he thought. This could never be the answer. But it would be foolish to deny that it had its uses.

Deliberately he began to mix a drink, making it very much stronger than the ones he had drunk before.

This would be the anodyne to his grief. This, by dulling that acute and sensitive awareness which was so great a part of his nature, would help him to endure this unending and almost unendurable torment. This might even give him, if only temporarily, the strength and the courage to fight, to plan, to scheme—at least to begin to force himself to climb out of that unspeakable abyss of blackness and despair.

He drained half the contents of the tumbler in one gigantic swallow and lit a cigarette.

The acrid blue smoke mingled unhappily and reluctantly with the fumes of burnt stew which still lingered in the room, but he smelt neither. He emptied his glass and began to mix another drink.

He must fight Conrad Roche. Suddenly he remembered what he had been unable to recall when he first opened the front door. The man's features reminded him with startling similarity of a bust of one of the Roman emperors he had once seen in a museum. Here were the same fleshy and sensual arrogance, the same dominant power in line of nose and jaw and the same tranquil and massive acceptance of mastery in the high and noble brow.

A Roman emperor with a modern empire. They had altered and influenced the lives and destinies of whole nations with votes in the Senate, implemented and enforced by the inexorable efficiency of the legions, the supreme fighting-machine of its age. He manipulated and probably even killed individuals who opposed him with the power of money.

But not all the tribes had accepted the rule of Rome. Many had fought, with primitive weapons, against the iron discipline of the cohorts. Many had fought and died, but as a result many more lived free in the hills and mountains and forests until as the centuries passed the legions were compelled to build walls and forts, behind which they could find shelter and safety.

He too, would fight.

But how? With what weapons? What

could he do? He was being watched, by people he did not know and therefore could not recognize. His every movement would be reported to Roche.

But he could telephone. There has hardly been time to put a tap on his telephone, and besides, no one had called at the flat, apart from Roche himself, since his official appointment to the case that morning. Otherwise Germaine would have told him.

He would telephone M. le Chef and tell him very briefly what had happened.

He glanced at his watch and sighed. At this hour M. le Chef was almost certainly engaged in frenetic copulations with his housemaid in the huge and ornate double bed, since this was the season of the year, he reflected ruefully, for wives to visit their cousins....

Although he knew well from past and bitter experience that there was an extension telephone in the master bedroom of the manorhouse, he was also well aware of the reception that invariably greeted a caller whose news or message was not of greater importance than that of what was actually happening at that precise moment beneath the vast and medieval canopy....

Nevertheless, he had to try. His news —the abduction of his wife as a method of cancelling and nullifying the official policy of the *Sûreté*—surely justified interrupting whatever excesses, perversions, contortions or variations on a sexual theme that could be imagined by an active and virile old *roué* of fabulous wealth.

No one would know that he had telephoned. And in the morning he would report to the office at his usual time and in the normal way. His unknown watchers would relay this information and Roche should conclude that he had gone there in order to ask that he be taken off the case.

If he did—and the reasoning was logical—then his assumption would be completely wrong. He would be telling M. le Chef—who in spite of his sexual aberrations was an extremely shrewd, astute and competent individual—every detail of what had actually happened and then they would talk it over and think out a plan of action.

He felt better now that he was trying to

think constructively rather than brooding and remembering and sorrowing at the pain and the injustice of what was happening to him.

He got up, went into the hall and made his telephone-call. He apologized swiftly for the interruption, and then told M. le Chef what had happened, recounting the facts briefly and concisely, and condensing his interview and conversation with Roche into two sentences. He concluded by adding:

'And I have been thinking that I had better come to the office at the usual time, as I am being watched. May I see you, m'sieu, as soon after that as you can manage?'

M. le Chef's voice was unwontonly gentle and considerate.

'I am very sorry indeed, Pinaud, to hear news like this—thank you for letting me know so soon. Come straight up to my office as soon as you arrive. I shall be waiting for you.'

'Thank you, m'sieu. I am grateful.'

M. Pinaud felt even better as he replaced the receiver. That would be a great help. No time would be wasted. To gether they would think of something.

Back in the kitchen he found that the absinthe bottle was empty. Perhaps, with rising costs, they were making them smaller these days.

It would be advisable, Pinaud, he told himself sternly, to make yourself some black coffee. You have had a hard day and tomorrow you may well have a harder one. You must therefore sleep—you need to sleep—

He filled the percolator with water, added coffee and lit the flame beneath. He put milk, sugar and a cup and saucer on a tray which he took to the table. And since in his opinion coffee without brandy was far worse than an egg without salt or ham without mustard, he found one of the two brandy bottles that were kept for great occasions at the bottom of the larder and brought one of them and a glass to the table as well.

And all the time he was doing this the words—to sleep—to sleep—were resounding and reverberating through his mind. How could he sleep—after what had happened? Where could he sleep—after the way that inhuman bastard had chosen to put him out of action?

The brandy might answer the first question—if he took enough. Whatever he drank would be preferable to taking sleeping-pills. After his telephone-call he could not be late at the office. Far better to wake up in good time with a splitting headache and a hangover than to take enough sleeping-pills to have any effect, to oversleep and to keep M. le Chef waiting.

To sleep—to sleep—but where? Not in their bed—where the memories would come again, tender and grieving, poignant and wistful—heart-breaking in their sweet and nostalgic vividness....

He carried the tray into the dining room.

In the cold grey light of the dawn he awoke with a strangled snore, slumped in the armchair, the brandy bottle uncorked but mercifully upright beneath him, the carpet stained and littered with spilt coffee and the shards of his broken cup.

CHAPTER 4

M. Pinaud was early to work, but M. le Chef had kept his word and was even earlier.

In that beautiful room on the first floor there were two chairs drawn up in front of the magnificent ormolu desk, a sight that M. Pinaud, in all his years of service, had never seen before.

A man was sitting in one of them. He stood up quickly in one lithe and controlled movement as soon as M. Pinaud came in. M. le Chef did not get up but waved his hand in greeting.

'Good morning, Pinaud,' he said. 'Permit me to introduce Charles Brancard, from the *Sûreté* in Marseilles.'

'It is my privilege,' Brancard said quietly as he held out his hand.

His clasp was firm and strong. M. Pinaud muttered something polite and motioned him back to the chair. Then he sat down himself on the other one and looked at him with an interest engendered by his knowledge that M. le Chef never did anything without a reason.

Brancard was tall and slim, with wide and powerful shoulders and a narrow fighter's waist. He moved with a controlled and almost animal grace and looked immensely strong. His skin was tanned as brown as leather and his clear eyes were of a startling light grey.

M. le Chef, having paused as if to marshal his thoughts, now cleared his throat and continued.

'I was very sorry to hear what you had to tell me last night on the telephone, Pinaud—so sorry and upset that I quite forgot to ask you if the children are all right.'

'Yes, thank you, m'sieu. They are with my wife's parents at Passy.'

'Good—good. I am glad to hear that. I have already explained the situation to Brancard here. He has been seconded to us from Marseilles and has just arrived. I propose to lend him to you unofficially —that is why I asked him to join us and meet you now. No one knows yet that he is here—and certainly not Roche and his associates. Consequently you will see that there are certain advantages in having him working with you. I should think he can be of great help. He can tail Roche and find out where he goes—which obviously you do not dare to do.'

'Naturally,' M. Pinaud assented. 'That is a very good idea. I am grateful, m'sieu.'

'It is the only logical thing to do,' said Brancard. His voice was crisp and assured. 'You personally, M'sieu Pinaud, cannot do anything except wait.'

'I know.' M. Pinaud agreed, very slowly and very quietly, tensing with a sudden and almost uncontrollable emotion. 'But not for long. I cannot afford to wait. My imagination will not let me wait.'

For a moment their silence was sympathetic. Then Brancard, tactfully, spoke to M. le Chef.

'Where does this Roche character live, m'sieu?'

'I believe he has a town house at St Germain des Prés. We can easily find out.'

'Good. We should do that. I could get

90

inside there as an electrician—tell them I have come to check on a faulty main switch or something like that. You can fix me up with a uniform and credentials, I am sure, m'sieu.'

'Of course.'

'I can act—gossip with the servants—that sort of thing. At least I should be able to find out whether he has taken Madame Pinaud there. If not, then I start to follow Roche wherever he goes. He is bound to keep in contact with her in some way.'

The man's confidence and evident competence were not only reassuring to M. Pinaud but definitely comforting.

'Yes,' he agreed quickly. 'That, too, is logical. And that is something you can do, but I do not dare.'

'Right,' said M. le Chef. 'Let us hope you get some results.'

'I will,' replied Brancard confidently. 'You know,' he went on, 'we have heard about this Roche in Marseilles.'

'But I thought he operated from here—'

'He does. But apparently he has over-reached himself recently in one of his giant mergers and now needs really big money very quickly. There had been rumours that he is mixed up in some huge heroin deal. This comes usually in our province, as you know, and although there is no evidence or proof yet, we have our own sources of information down there about anything to do with heroin. And what we get to know is usually accurate.'

'Yes,' put in M. Pinaud eagerly. 'That confirms what Yvette Rostand told me. You know about her and her husband's body—'

'Yes,' interrupted M. le Chef. 'I put Brancard in the picture before you came. What did you learn from her?'

'Not a great deal, m'sieu. But what there was might be important. She confirmed that there had been friction between her husband and Roche over some deal or scheme with which he did not agree. I will let you have a full report as soon as I have time. This heroin business would tie up with the wharf at Mitterand.'

'Obviously. You said on the telephone that you had been there?'

'Yes. I went yesterday after interviewing her and nearly got killed. They were either expecting me—although I fail to see how anyone could have known—or are always there as a permanent guard. And yet there was nothing in the warehouse. I checked very carefully. The barge was empty.'

'If he is going to use that barge for shipping his cargo,' put in Brancard, 'He would obviously hide the heroin somewhere else, not in a place connected with him, until he is ready. But the barge is essential and must be available when he wants it. That would explain the guard.'

'I will organize a twenty-four hour watch on that wharf,' said M. le Chef, 'And let you know what happens.'

'Perhaps nothing will happen,' said Brancard, 'Now that his guards are dead. He may change his plans.'

'It would be simpler for him to replace the guards,' interposed M. Pinaud quickly. 'I have an idea that barge is important.'

'That is the point of the watch,' M. le Chef told him. 'We shall know if and when he moves it, and when I get the river-police to co-operate we can find out where.'

'Good,' said Brancard. 'I can do a shift on that watch.'

M. Pinaud nodded.

M. le Chef looked from one to the other.

'Now then,' he continued. 'Have we any other ideas? Is there anything else we can do?'

He leaned back in his chair. Brancard shook his head. M. Pinaud opened his mouth, began to speak and then closed it again firmly. M. le Chef looked at him questioningly and curiously, and when he resumed speaking, his voice was unwontedly gentle.

'I agree with Brancard that for the moment, Pinaud, there is nothing for you to do. I will get Brancard organized at once. Just now, we depend on him and what he can find out at St Germain.'

M. Pinaud stood up as though impelled by some giant spring.

'There is one thing I can do,' he said quietly to M. le Chef.

Then he turned to Brancard and held out his hand, and his smile was one that his employer had very rarely seen.

'My thoughts and my good wishes will be with you,' he said simply. 'Wherever you go and whatever you do.'

Brancard was on his feet as M. Pinaud turned to him. They shook hands.

'Thank you,' he replied. 'I will do my best.'

'What are you going to do, Pinaud?' asked M. le Chef, a trifle testily. He had a vague and irritating impression that the control of this situation was no longer in his hands.

M. Pinaud began to say something and then he changed his mind. He considered for a long moment before answering the question.

'I am going out through the back door, m'sieu, into the tradesmen's entrance of the new block of flats. Then I shall walk to the front door and ask the porter to get me a taxi to the Métro station. Even if Roche's friends are watching this building it is not likely that they will be able to follow me to the platform of St Michel.'

M. le Chef stared.

'But what on earth for?'

Once more M. Pinaud considered the question. Then he replied slowly and deliberately, choosing his words with care.

'I have been thinking about this, m'sieu, ever since last night—not impersonally because that is impossible—but trying to get the right perspective, and I have come to the conclusion that it would be far better if I do not tell you or anyone what I am going to do.'

Had M. Pinaud paused there, he was sure that M. le Chef would have said something. He could see the mouth opposite already opening, forming the words. He therefore continued quickly, without any interval.

'I have a clue—the slenderest and most tenuous of clues. But it must mean something. It has got to mean something. And it is all I have. Therefore I must follow it. This is something I must do myself. To find my wife is too important to leave to anyone else.'

He finished speaking and for a long moment there was silence.

At length M. le Chef nodded his head slowly, as if finally understanding.

'And then—' he began quietly.

M. Pinaud looked at him directly. His powerful figure straightened. Some great force seemed to transform him, transcending the depression and desolation that had so obviously belittled him throughout the interview. M. le Chef found it hard to meet his eyes.

'Then,' he replied, very slowly and very quietly, 'after my wife is home with me—then I will talk to Roche myself.'

M. le Chef shivered. Brancard looked very thoughtful.

* * * *

The enormous concrete building was new and rectangular. It towered up into the sky, overshadowing even the latest high-rise efforts in Montparnasse, supported apparently on what looked like four slender stilts.

M. Pinaud stood for a moment and stared up at the almost unbelievable height. As the soft white clouds swam gently across the sky he had the illusion that the whole massive building was floating with them and he felt the first sensations of vertigo.

How could those four slender pillars continue to support all that weight?

He knew that he was being stupid and old-fashioned. He knew very well that pilings had been driven down deep into the sub-soil and that mathematical calculations, checked with infinite care, had probably proved that each pillar, of reinforced steel and concrete, could well take the whole weight by itself, but nevertheless, to him it seemed all wrong.

He liked his buildings to grow out of the earth on which they had been meant to stand. He liked castles with keeps and bastions and baileys, he liked medieval manor-houses set in a fold of the land and he liked the magnificent town-houses in St Germain des Prés. But this building was a nightmare. This was—

Then he remembered that he was here for a purpose.

He climbed the broad shallow steps two at a time. Beside the wide entrance a black marble slab bore the words 'Roche Enterprises', engraved deeply and artistically and filled with gold paint.

Inside he found himself in a vast entrance-hall furnished with elegant austerity and supreme good taste. A reception desk and telephone switchboard were at the far end. An attractive blonde girl smiled at him encouragingly as he began to walk towards her. One wall was lined with comfortable armchairs, spaced at discreet intervals. Beside each one stood a small cabinet containing directories and with a telephone on the table-top.

He put on his best smile to match hers.

'Good morning, mademoiselle. My name is Lebrun—Hector Lebrun. I suppose I am too early for M'sieu Roche?'

She could not know from his expression or manner that he was literally holding his breath, waiting for her answer. Everything depended on it.

Her smile deepened. She glanced at the electric clock on the wall.

'By at least an hour, M'sieu Lebrun. His first appointment is not until ten-thirty. And he never sees anyone without an appointment.'

He contrived to look disappointed, discouraged and perplexed, all at the same time.

'Is there anyone else who could help you?' she continued brightly.

He considered for a moment. She must be made to understand that this was a very important decision.

'Yes,' he said finally. 'I am sure you can yourself. Do you think I could just have a few moments' conversation with his personal secretary? I have a message for him which is a little complicated. It would be more satisfactory if I explained it verbally and not on the telephone.'

'Of course, m'sieu. I suggest the best thing is for you to take one of the lifts over there to the fifteenth floor, where M'sieu Roche's offices are located. I will telephone one of his secretaries, Madame Arnaud, that you are on your way up to see her.'

He thanked her very politely and walked to the bank of express lifts.

* * * *

On the fifteenth floor, a door opposite the lift, on the other side of the corridor, was open.

A girl was standing in the entrance

waiting for him.

'M'sieu Lebrun?' she asked and smiled. 'I am Janice Arnaud, personal secretary to M'sieu Roche. Please come in.'

'Thank you.'

In one swift glance he confirmed his first impressions that the standards of the employment of Conrad Roche's female staff must have been motivated by certain very definite principles.

Her features and figure were beautiful. Her hair was of that unique shade of coppery red found once in a lifetime. She wore a lime-green dress with a plunging neckline. His height enabled him to see almost down to her navel. The sunlight through a large window behind her made it obvious that she wore nothing beneath her dress.

He wondered if there was a Monsieur Arnaud, and, if so, what he thought about it all.

The office was large, sound-proofed and air-conditioned, and both tastefully and luxuriously furnished. Set in the far wall, a door led to another room. A series of exquisitely framed etchings adorned one wall, and his boots sank deeply into the pile of the fitted carpet.

'Take a chair, M'sieu Lebrun,' she said, seating herself behind the desk. 'I understand that you have a message for M'sieu Roche?'

'Thank you.'

He sat down and smiled at her.

'Yes, madame, that is correct. But since I have been informed that he only sees visitors by appointment and as my message is rather a complicated one, I came to the conclusion in the lift that the simplest thing for me to do would be to make an appointment myself—would you agree?'

'Of course.'

She reached for a massive leather-bound desk-diary.

'Now let me see—' she began.

'I am sorry to interrupt you,' he said suddenly. 'But the other day I was introduced to Yvette Rostand. She told me she was also personal secretary to M'sieu Roche—is she in today?'

She looked up at him with a wet and lascivious smile.

'She was quite right. M'sieu Roche has

five personal secretaries. But she is not in today. She is ill. I have just had that pitiful old father of hers in here wasting my time asking where she was—if she had come to work. I told him no—how would I know where she is? Now, M'sieu Lebrun, would tomorrow morning suit you, at eleven o'clock?'

In a few brief instants he took to consider, many other thoughts flashed through M. Pinaud's mind. He wanted to tell this mindless body that no man concerned with the welfare and the happiness of his daughter could be considered pitiful, but surely became worthy of admiration. But even as he thought he resisted the impulse. It was doubtful if he could ever make her understand.

Besides, in trying to penetrate her mental processes, he might so easily upset her—and he still needed her for more information. He had not yet even asked her the vital question—the question that was far more important to him even than his sense of justice or his pity and compassion for Victor Marvin.

'That will be fine,' he said. 'Just a moment—let me check—'

He took out his pocket-book, opened it and studied the back of his unpaid gas-bill with a frowning concentration.

'Yes—yes,' he continued. 'I can be here at eleven. Tell him I shall only take a few moments of his valuable time.'

'I am afraid I must ask the purpose of the interview—'

He did not hesitate.

'Of course. Tell him it is very personal and confidential—about my daughter—I am sure he will be interested.'

'Very well, m'sieu.'

He stood up and crossed over to where she sat, writing in the diary. Nearer and above her, the view was even better.

'Thank you so much for all your help, Madame Arnaud. I am most grateful.'

Again he smiled at her. And M. Pinaud's smile, even when filtered through a hangover, was something very few people could resist.

Janice Arnaud was no exception. As she told her favourite girl-friend that evening in a hectic and breathless outpouring of confidences—since M. Arnaud's brief but glorious tenure of that exquisite body had ceased abruptly, even though the use of his name lingered on, when he found her in bed with his chauffeur—after all, my dear, it is not too bad having a respectable type like that looking down your dress—you never know what it might lead to—some morons I know have done pretty well for themselves using that technique—and to be perfectly honest and truthful I did buy it at an outrageous price for that very reason—but he was so nice about it all, this one—so strong and yet I am sure so gentle—his eyes were filled with lust—but then he is a man—and how I knew that he would never hurt you or ask you to do disgusting things—he would have been fair and honest—these things seemed to shine out of his eyes even over and above the lust....

She smiled up at him brightly, arching her magnificent body provocatively.

'The name is Janice,' she said very softly.

'Most grateful indeed, Janice,' he repeated dutifully, bending even lower and placing one hand on the arm of her chair. 'Perhaps if you are not too busy, my dear Janice, after I have seen M'sieu Roche tomorrow, we could have lunch together and discuss a few things I am sure you will find interesting.'

'Thank you very much,' she replied. 'I would like that. But I am afraid I can only let you know definitely tomorrow when you come. By then we shall know the day's programme.'

'Of course.'

He straightened up. Now was the time. It was now or never.

'Now I must go. I shall look forward to seeing you Janice, tomorrow—far more than meeting M'sieu Roche at eleven o'clock. Oh—by the way—I thought I saw him at Maxim's the other day with the celebrated surgeon Dr Parmentier. They have their photographs in the newpapers so often these days that I recognized them both at once. Does he know the famous Dr Parmentier from La Salpétrière?'

Janice Arnaud looked puzzled, which was not surprising. M. Pinaud held his breath, his mind already racing ahead feverishly, prepared to lead the conversation immediately and without hesitation into whatever direction her reply indicated.

She shook her head slowly and reluctantly, obviously unhappy that she could not agree.

'No—no—I don't think so—'

She paused for a moment, thinking. M. Pinaud waited silently, controlling the rising tension within him with an iron self-restraint, until even he could stand it no longer.

She had said no. She was not saying anything more. He would have to take it on from there. He opened his mouth and then closed it again as she began to speak. His sigh of relief was inaudible but he knew that he had won.

'The only doctor M'sieu Roche knows is his very good friend Albert Vaucluse. I was thinking so hard just now because I was trying to remember if I had ever heard M'sieu Roche mention that he knew anyone at the hospital but I am sure he never has. You must have been mistaken, M'sieu Lebrun.'

He laughed easily, through sheer relief.

'I probably was. Newspaper photographs are notoriously bad. In any case —it is not important. Not nearly so important as the fact that we are going to have lunch together. *Au revoir,* Janice— and thank you once again for your help.'

He bowed himself out and took the express-lift down to the reception hall. There he thanked the blonde receptionist once again very politely and then left the building.

Outside he forced himself to walk slowly. A man in a hurry was always conspicuous. It was not likely that his unknown watchers had followed him here but he could not be too careful. Too much was at stake.

He walked for a few blocks, turning left and right until he was in the Avenue St Martin and well away from Roche's building.

Half-way down the avenue was a large *café* with gaily-striped awnings and outside tables. He went through the open doors to the room inside, where the telephone would be nearer.

Even there, having ordered a coffee, he forced himself to wait, watching the people outside through the plate-glass windows, to see if he recognized anyone as having been following him.

CHAPTER 5

'Yes, Pinaud?'

M. le Chef's voice was peevish and irritable. Someone or something had upset him. M. Pinaud sighed inaudibly, controlled his impatience and forced politeness into his voice.

'I am sorry to disturb you, m'sieu, but I need some information quickly. Would you be good enough to help me?'

'Everyone seems to need everything quickly, Pinaud. There are only twelve hours in a working day, as you probably know.'

This was not going to be easy. He wondered what had happened.

'Of that I am fully aware, m'sieu. But in this case speed is vital. The clue I have been following—'

'The clue you would not divulge to us this morning,' M. le Chef interrupted in an acid and disparaging tone and with a complete lack of enthusiasm.

Was that it? M. Pinaud wondered. Had that upset him?

'I still think it was for the best, m'sieu,' he replied patiently. 'Now I have a lead. The name is Vaucluse—Albert Vaucluse. He is either a doctor or a surgeon and he must be practising somewhere near, either in the city or in one of the suburbs. I must have his address at once—'

'Impossible, Pinaud. A search like that could take hours.'

'Surely the list of medical practitioners—'

'Vaucluse is a common name.'

'Agreed, m'sieu—but comparatively few are doctors.'

'Paris is a large city. Do you know how many—'

At this juncture M. Pinaud could no longer control his impatience and not only lost his temper but also committed the unpardonable sin of interrupting his chief in the middle of his conversation.

'I don't care a four-letter word how large it is, m'sieu. May I point out very respectfully that my wife has been kidnapped and this Vaucluse is almost cer-

110

tainly the man who is keeping her a prisoner. Roche boasted that he is the one who will send me parts of her body. Now I am in a *café* on the Avenue St Martin in Montparnasse waiting until I know where to go. Would you call me back here as soon as you possibly can.'

He read off the number from the base of the telephone and then waited, not without some trepidation.

There was a long silence. When M. le Chef spoke at last, his voice was completely different.

'Very well, Pinaud. Wait there. I will do my best.'

M. Pinaud sighed with relief, thanked him very sincerely, replaced the receiver and went back to his coffee.

* * * *

The minutes dragged like hours.

Perhaps he ought to have a brandy. He needed a brandy. He felt that it was essential he should have two or three large brandies. After all, what was coffee without brandy?

He did not waste time in answering his

own rhetorical question but signalled the waiter instead.

Then he emptied the glass eagerly, called for another and then thought briefly about M. le Chef and what an extraordinary man he was.

In the years of their long association together he himself had been insulted, vilified, hindered, frustrated, hampered, criticized, obstructed, censured, even deliberately thwarted—but never once had M. le Chef let him down.

There was a first time for everything. He hoped and prayed that it was not going to be now. Too much depended on this information.

He looked at his watch. It might have stopped. He checked it by the clock on the wall. The watch was still going.

All the tables near him were occupied. It seemed that the whole world came into a *café* for a drink. His hearing was extraordinarily acute; without wishing to, he could not help overhearing other people's conversations.

At the next table a swarthy and ferocious looking individual was drinking absinthe with a lady. She was older—

considerably older—than him, and once had been extremely beautiful. Now her face was ravaged with grief, her eyes red with sorrow.

'I told you when we started it could not last—'

'I did not believe you. I could not believe you. You took something that was dead and you made it come alive again—'

'Maybe I did—but all the same—'

'We have been good for each other —we have felt the earth move underneath us—'

'I know—but I told you—'

'And what about Adrienne—a twelve-year-old? You have been a father to her—'

'I am not concerned with Adrienne. Neither am I involved. It is you I went to bed with. She was something you brought along with you. I did my best. A good kid—'

'Is that all? She worships you—'

'Then she will be due for a shock—'

M. Pinaud drank another brandy. He tried not to think.

At the table the other side an old

white-haired couple were seated, sharing a carafe of wine. They sat strangely, poignantly still, sad and suffering, but resigned. The old man's hand, blue-veined and swollen with arthritis, held one of hers on the table all the time they spoke.

'I can't understand why they did not tell him—'

'They never tell them—'

'Then why tell us?'

'Because we are his parents, and they have to tell someone—'

'But it seems so—so unfair—'

'What can they do? They cut him open and are ready to operate. It is their job. They know what to do. Then they find this. They know they would be wasting their time. At least he can have another six months. So they sew him up again and tell him that everything is all right but he should take care—'

'But it is more than unfair—it is monstrous—that we should know this and not him—'

'What would you do, dear—if you knew that you had only six months to live? Would it make you happy? At least he is at peace. He thinks the operation was successful. He has something to occupy his mind—taking care of himself —and he believes—'

'What about us—'

'We are old, dear. We have learnt to endure. We have come nearly to the end. For us it is not so important—'

'To know and not to be able to tell—'

'This is our duty. We undertook, an obligation when we created him. Our obligation has lasted longer, that is all—'

It was difficult not to think. He tried to empty his mind of thought, since thought about her was torment. Even as he tried he knew that it was impossible. She was part of him, part of his very being, part of his life....

At an adjoining table a young man spoke urgently and fiercely, and then even more urgently and more fiercely to the girl beside him, in the intervals of replenishing her glass from a giant bottle with a very suspicious-looking label. The wine was an extraordinary shade of red. It reminded him of dog's blood.

'I tell you, there is nothing to it. I have been watching him for weeks. He shuts

the shop every night and then puts pad-
locks on the outsides of both doors, front
and back. So he has to go up this outside
iron ladder to get to his flat. I have seen
him do it. And he always carries this
large brown envelope in his hand. It must
be money—'

He was dark-haired and dark-eyed,
small but extremely tough, with a droop-
ing moustache and a high-necked swea-
ter. She was thin and fair and pale, pretty
in a colourless and vapid way, and just
now obviously terrified.

'Why doesn't he lock it up in his safe
then—he must have a safe if it is a jewel-
lery shop—'

'I don't know. I don't care. Perhaps
he only has insurance for stock and not
for cash. Perhaps he feels safer with it
under his pillow. Perhaps he likes to
count it—what the hell does it matter?
All you have got to do is to swear that I
have been with you all the evening—that
is to say, from six o'clock on instead of
from eight, when I shall come—'

'Supposing someone sees you come in
at eight—'

'Don't be a fool. I shall wait until the

116

coast is clear—'

'I don't like it—'

'I know you don't like it. I am sick and tired of hearing you say that you don't like it and that you don't want anything to do with it. But all the same you are going to do it—because this is our big chance. Then we can go away together—'

He wondered what lies—in ornate and coloured script—had been printed on that label. Surely there could not be vintage years for dog's blood. He ordered more coffee. He drank more brandy. He forced himself to keep calm and wait.

Next to them sat an interesting couple. The man was young and handsome, with pale, sensitive and aquiline features framed in a neat and pointed beard. His hair was long and silken, and fell down over his shoulders. The delicate and haunting fragility of his face reminded M. Pinaud of a medieval portrait of one of the disciples by an early Italian master. He wore a belted blanket and trousers thrust into knee-high boots.

The girl beside him was beautiful, but she looked ill. Her face was white and strained with an air of sickness, and dark

shadows circled her deep brown eyes.
She was exquisitely and expensively dressed.

She was drinking champagne. The
bottle stood in an ice-bucket beside her.
The man was drinking orange-juice.

'I tell you I know someone who will do
it—first-class qualifications—and completely discreet—'

'I don't care who you know—and I
still say I am going to have it—'

'You must be mad—'

'That could be. I must have been mad
to have loved you. But I did. And I still
do. And so when you go—as I know you
will now—at least I shall still have something left to remember you—'

'I told you it is a sin—'

'You are the one who is mad. To create
a child is a miracle, not a sin—'

'Try to keep your mind logical and not
feminine. I was trying to say that it is a
sin to bring a child into this world as it is
today—a nuclear war is inevitable—the
rehearsals have already started—half the
fertile soil will be a cratered waste—there
will be only enough food for a quarter of
the population—racial massacres on a

global scale—black and yellow against white—'

'You do not frighten me—'

'Use your imagination—use your intellect—'

'I prefer to use my courage. For a little while we were happy together. We made a heaven on this earth. You are good at taking. But love is more than taking— love means giving as well. You are not and never have been prepared to give. I am. By giving I shall keep a little of that happiness. You have already lost it all. And so I must pity you as well as love you—'

There were tears in her eyes. She ignored them, lifted the bottle from the ice and refilled her glass.

She has courage, that one, he reflected. If he really loved her he would have partaken of it. She has enough for two.

All the world, it seemed, had problems as well as him, his thoughts ran on. But he could do nothing about his. He could only wait, the tension and anxiety surging up within him in a nauseating wave. Never had he known that minutes could be so long.

Again he ordered coffee and brandy. There was nothing else to do. Perhaps it would have been cheaper to have bought the bottle, he reflected.

Then he shut his eyes so that he would not have to look at all those people. The sight of them suddenly depressed him.

But with his eyes closed it seemed that he heard even more acutely, and the phrases began to follow each other so rapidly that sometimes they intermingled and then he could no longer understand.

'But she is only twelve—'

'Plenty of time to grow up into a tart—'

'We shall have to be so careful all the time—'

'We must never let him suspect—'

'Who said anything about killing him—'

'If you don't he will recognize and identify you—'

'When you have learnt to give—come back to me and be a father to your son. In spite of all your prophecies of doom the world will still be here—and so will I —so will he—'

120

* * * *

When the bell eventually rang from the telephone on the wall he was out of his chair and grasping the receiver before the proprietor had even begun to move from his stool.

'Hullo—'

'Pinaud?'

'Yes, m'sieu.'

'Albert Vaucluse operates a small and very exclusive clinic in the Bois de Boulogne, Avenue St Cloud Fourteen.'

'Thank you very much, m'sieu. May I ask what kind of clinic?'

'Dr Vaucluse seems to specialize only in very wealthy private patients who have problems either with drink or drugs or both. A sufficient number of them have died whilst under his care for our Narcotics Squad to become quite interested. There have been rumours and talk and gossip, apparently—enough for them to keep an eye on him, but so far no proof. He is reputed to be a very successful man and is probably making a fortune. Just the type to be a friend of Roche, although no one seems to have known this.'

The curt incisive voice ceased.

'I am very grateful, m'sieu,' M. Pinaud said with great sincerity in his voice, 'for your quick and most efficient help. If I owe you an apology for not taking you into my confidence, please accept it now. Roche boasted when he threatened me that he had a friend who specialized in the kind of surgery that would enable him to post portions of my wife's body to me if I did not obey him. I did not mean to make an issue or a mystery of it, but I am sure you will understand that in a personal matter such as this—'

'Of course, Pinaud—of course.'

The voice in his ear was now gentle and kind.

'Think and say no more about it. I quite understand. How you ever got his name—without seeing Roche—is a miracle. You must tell me about the achievement when I see you. I presume you are going over there now?'

'At once, m'sieu.'

'Good. You never waste time. But just now wait a little longer. Brancard has just collected your new car. I propose to

send him over with it now to your flat—
you may need it for a quick get-away. Besides, two are always better than one in
such a situation. He can cover for you.
He could be a help.'

'Thank you, m'sieu—but not the flat.
I lost Roche's watchers in the Métro this
morning, so they will probably go back
there to wait for my return. Ask him to
stop outside the Café du Roi in the Avenue St Martin and pick me up.'

'Very well, Pinaud. Wait for him—he
should not be long. But don't go there
alone—whatever you do. These are dangerous people.'

'Very well, m'sieu.'

'Right. Good-bye for now—and good
luck.'

'Thank you once again, m'sieu. Good-
bye.'

* * * *

Brancard came into the *café* quickly,
saw him at once and walked over to the
table. He glanced at the pile of mats
beside the empty glass and the coffee-
pot, but when he spoke it was about

something else.

'There is no parking outside. Nor anywhere near. I drove round the block twice. We had better be quick.'

M. Pinaud laid a note on the table and together they left the *café*.

The car was outside, new and shining, sleek and gleaming, the latest model. Normally, M. Pinaud's heart would have been filled with joy and pride in his new possession, to say nothing of gratitude towards M. le Chef for his efficiency and understanding. Now he was not interested.

Brancard handed him the keys.

'You drive. It is your car.'

M. Pinaud shrugged.

'Yes. I suppose so.'

He unlocked the door and slipped into the driving-seat. Brancard sat down beside him. The controls were familiar and nearly all in the same places. He studied them for a few moments and then started the engine. He adjusted the seat a little further back and then let in the clutch smoothly, heading for the Porte d'Auteuil and the Bois de Boulogne.

Beneath his impassive countenance the many facets of his complex character were engaged in a typical conflict. All he wanted to do was to put his foot down hard and get to the clinic of Dr Vaucluse as soon as he possibly could, there to find and rescue his wife. And yet he could no more ill-use a new and so exquisitely complicated piece of machinery as this car than he could bring himself to strike a child—to one of his nature to do either of these things was impossible and unthinkable.

He tried to explain something of this to Brancard without taking his eyes off the road.

'With a new engine the first few hours of running are the most important. Revolutions and speed do not matter so much—this is how the engine is designed to function—but strain can be fatal.'

Brancard nodded without answering. He was either lost in admiration or stupefied with terror. There were grounds for both. Just at that moment M. Pinaud was sliding his new car swiftly with literally centimetres to spare on either side between a swaying and culpably overloaded bus and a thundering sixteen-wheeled lorry.

M. Pinaud drove on, concentrating on achieving the most successful compromise between his conflicting principles—accelerating smoothly, always on indirect gear, to gain the best response from the powerful engine, sensing unerringly and instinctively, with a competence gained from years of experience, the right gap in the line of the traffic ahead, and anticipating many of the approaching drivers' reactions well before they obeyed them.

Brancard very wisely did not distract him. He did not speak until they reached the Avenue St Cloud and M. Pinaud visibly relaxed.

Then he stirred in his seat, took out a packet of cigarettes, offered it to M. Pinaud and paid him a very charming compliment.

'Well,' he said quietly, settling back in his seat and blowing out the lighter he had touched to both their cigarettes, 'I always thought I knew how to handle a car—but after this morning I know now that I have a lot to learn.'

M. Pinaud was pleased.

'Thank you,' he replied. 'Mind you—I have been at it for a long time.'

Then he concentrated on reading the numbers on the gate-posts. These were set at impressive intervals and distinguished the large and luxuriously detached houses, each one set well back from the road, screened and sometimes almost completely hidden in a profusion of trees and shrubs.

Number fourteen was almost at the end of the avenue on the left-hand side of the road. There was no sign or name beside the number.

He drove past the entrance-gates, pulled up on his side and switched off the engine.

'Before we start,' said Brancard, 'I must tell you that I had no luck at St Germain. I went there early this morning. I got in all right. I did everything except make love to the maid. I flattered the housekeeper so much that she offered me a drink and I impressed some male secretary with all my technical knowledge. I went right through that house from cellars to attics, on the pretext of tracing the faulty wiring—but all for nothing. Your wife is not there, M'sieu Pinaud—I am sorry.'

M. Pinaud blew out a vast cloud of smoke.

'Thank you,' he said again. 'But there is no need to be sorry. I know where she is.'

Now that the prospect of action was imminent he felt better. His voice was brisk and assured, almost cheerful.

Brancard stared.

'Where?'

'Here. In this house, number fourteen, the private clinic of Dr Vaucluse, friend of Conrad Roche, kidnapper.'

There was something in the way he pronounced these words, very slowly and very carefully, that caused Brancard to tense in his seat.

'The chief said that you had found out his name and that he had got this address for you. And that you intended going there. But he also said that you had no proof. How can you be sure—'

M. Pinaud shrugged and interrupted him.

'I don't know how. But I am quite

128

sure—'

M. Pinaud shrugged and interrupted him.

'I don't know how. But I am quite sure. Instinct, perhaps. And yet instinct in this case is not really necessary. Quite apart from the information he inadvertently gave me about his surgeon friend, this is the logical place to keep her—not too far from Roche at St Germain and in a private clinic for drug-addicts and alcoholics, which almost certainly has a staff of fairly tough male nurses and bars on most of the windows. It all adds up.'

Then his voice changed.

'Now if you would get out and open those gates, see that they are securely held and leave them open, I will back the car into the drive in case we have to leave in a hurry.'

'Right.'

Lifting the door-latch, Brancard smiled.

'That is why he asked me to come with you,' he said as he got out.

M. Pinaud did not reply. He waited until both gates were open. Then he started the engine, looked both ways to see that the road was clear, and then reversed, swinging the car around skilfully in one wide sweep until he backed into the drive.

He stopped the car almost immediately, while it was still screened from the house by the trees and bushes. Then he got out and unbuttoned his jacket.

'I am going up the drive,' he said to Brancard, 'but you keep on the grass here—somewhere behind those trees. Find yourself a place where you can watch the house without being seen.'

'But—what are you going to do?'

'Nothing complicated,' replied M. Pinaud quietly. 'I am going to ring the front-door bell and announce myself as a new patient, very highly recommended. Once the door is open I am going in behind my gun to get her out. It does not really matter—nor do I care very much—what I have to do.'

Brancard hesitated.

'The odds are bad enough for two. We don't know how many there may be inside. To go in alone is suicide. Let me come with you.'

'No. Although I am grateful for the

offer. This is how it is going to be. You are quite right about the odds, but that does not matter. In these circumstances and in this situation, it is logical to separate. You can be of far more help to me as an outside cover. I shall have the advantage of surprise, once I am in, and so will you here, if you take care not to be seen. If anything happens to me and they try to get her out, you should have no trouble, because they will not be expecting you. Oh—and lend me your handcuffs. An extra pair might be useful.'

'But—'

'No arguments.'

His tone was flat, final and uncompromising.

Brancard shrugged, felt in his hip-pocket and handed over the handcuffs. M. Pinaud slipped them into his side-pocket and then continued:

'Now find yourself a good place. And above all, don't come in—even if you hear shooting and no one comes out. In that case, take the car and drive—no—it will be quicker to use the radio-telephone to get reinforcements. Understand?'

'Yes,' replied Brancard, 'I understand

all right. But I don't like it.'

He crouched and began to run with astonishing speed towards the copse of trees. Before he reached them he half-turned and called out over his shoulder:

'Good luck.'

M. Pinaud waved in acknowledgement and walked up the drive towards the clinic.

CHAPTER 6

The house at the end of the drive was large and imposing. Wide and tall windows on the ground floor and first floors denoted spacious and lofty rooms. The top floor, probably converted from the attics and loft, had several small windows, all heavily barred.

Money had been spent, lavishly and tastefully, on upkeep and maintenance, both of the house and the terraced gardens on either side. Rich and gleaming paint gave an opulent look to all the woodwork, the window-panes were crystal-clear and the cement in the mellow brickwork had been re-pointed with artistic skill. The lawns were smoothly cut, the flowers staked and the beds immaculately free from weeds and stones.

And yet—and yet, M. Pinaud thought sombrely as he rang the bell on the massive front door—the whole aspect of all that care and attention seemed somehow cold and repelling. This was not a happy house. Children would not have played and laughed and cried here. Boys had never churned and cut up that impeccable turf, happily kicking a football about. This house had never known the joy and happiness that—

The door opened quickly and noiselessly.

The man who stood on the threshhold was tall and powerfully built, with tough and craggy features. He wore a short-sleeved white smock, revealing huge and muscular forearms.

He may have been described, M. Pinaud reflected, as a male nurse on the personnel list of the clinic's employees, but the word thug would have been more apt....

Aloud, his voice radiated friendship, cordiality and goodwill.

'Good morning to you. My name is Lebrun. My good friend Conrad Roche told me to come here and see Dr Vaucluse. Do you think he would be kind enough to spare me a few moments?'

The man's air of surly belligerence

changed visibly at the mention of the name Roche and he stepped back almost deferentially.

'Come in, m'sieu. I will see if—'

This was all that M. Pinaud needed—all that he had counted on by giving a false name and mentioning Roche and Vaucluse.

In a second he was over the threshold and the man's voice died as he looked down at the gun pointing so steadily at his stomach.

'Turn around,' M. Pinaud told him quietly, shutting the front door behind him with his other hand, 'and take me to Dr Vaucluse.'

Without a word the man obeyed and led the way across the heavily carpeted and spacious hall to a corridor at the far end.

M. Pinaud's reflections had been accurate. A male nurse, sufficiently well paid and loyal to his employer, might well have taken a chance, however desperate. But a thug, used to violence, knew that it does not pay to argue with a gun, especially when the man holding it has enough sense not to get too near.

The man knocked on the first door. M. Pinaud noticed—because he had been trained to notice such things—that it had a peculiar and complicated lock, but he had not time just then to think about it.

'Come in,' called a voice. The man pushed open the door and they walked into the office of Dr Vaucluse.

M. Pinaud gave him one swift glance. Dr Vaucluse was a small rat-like individual with a large nose and dissipated-looking features, dressed immaculately in a very expensive suit. He was seated behind a large and ornate desk on whose surface, littered with papers, letters, pamphlets and magazines, both his hands, palms down, were resting.

M. Pinaud gestured towards the back of a heavy wooden armchair on the other side of the room and jerked Brancard's handcuffs out of his side-pocket.

'Sit in it,' he said to the man in front of him. 'One hand under the arm and one over. Clasp them together.'

The man obeyed. Dr Vaucluse had not moved. M. Pinaud walked widely around the chair, still covering both the occupants of the room, and from behind snapped the handcuffs on his wrists with the other hand.

'May I ask—' began Dr Vaucluse mildly.

M. Pinaud came quickly to stand by the side of the desk, where he could watch the doctor and still see the open door. The armchair was heavy and solid, but the man in it looked immensely strong. It would not be wise to remain too near. The gun now covered the doctor.

'You may,' he interrupted hardly. 'My name is Pinaud and I have come for my wife.'

The doctor's hands were still open on the desk. M. Pinaud glanced swiftly around the room. He had the impression that it was tastefully and luxuriously furnished, but afterwards he could not have told you in what way.

The second unusual thing he noticed was the line of vents high up on the opposite wall, immediately below the ceiling.

'Indeed?' replied the doctor coolly. 'I am unarmed. And what are you prepared to do—'

'Anything—'

Again M. Pinaud interrupted him, and this time in his voice there was a menace and a restrained ferocity that caused the doctor to tense uneasily in his chair.

'Anything,' he repeated. 'And everything necessary. Shoot you, Dr Vaucluse, in the lower stomach or in the legs to splinter your knee-caps—extract one of your eyeballs with the foresight of this gun—and there are other things I can think of. This is my wife we are talking about. Dr Vaucluse—perhaps you would make a great effort and try to understand.'

As he finished speaking, two things happened simultaneously.

Two men in white smocks rushed silently into the room through the open doorway, and the handcuffed man, forcing up the heavy chair with a supreme effort, staggered across to join them.

* * * *

Without shifting his position, M. Pinaud pivoted on his left foot, and the first man caught his heavy right boot, sweeping up in a vicious *savate* kick, full in the groin. He collapsed like a deflated balloon.

A softening that was almost a smile touched M. Pinaud's lips as, still without changing his stance, he shot the second man in the shoulder and watched his fall with satisfaction.

Exhilaration flooded him like a wave. It was something even more than exhilaration—an ecstasy tinged with an almost demoniacal glee—and it seemed to surge up within him and flood him with the majesty of a breaking wave, engendering a power and a strength and an irresistible force to his actions that made him invincible.

These were the men who had been guarding his wife—who had probably insulted and humiliated her—who might even have ill-treated her—this was no more than they deserved.

Then he moved himself, far more quickly than either of them had done, and just avoided the clumsy rush of the man with the chair. The edge of his hand came down hard on the back of the man's neck as he passed and he went down, unconscious, with a crash that snapped one of the chair-legs off short.

He turned towards the desk and noticed two more things. The door was now shut and the doctor's hands were no longer visible.

As he raised the gun they reappeared quickly, still empty. The doctor drew back his cuff and examined the watch on his wrist. He nodded his head slowly, as if satisfied.

It was the last thing that M. Pinaud noticed that provided him with the key to the mystery and understanding of what was happening.

The watch was a chronograph. If the doctor had pressed the crown of the recording-hand some time previously, either before they had first entered his office, or later during the fight, then there would be an indication of the time elapsed since on the recording-dial.

The air suddenly seemed thicker and heavier, and he found that he had difficulty in focussing his eyes.

He made a great effort to control his swimming senses and to add up the facts into a coherent and logical pattern. The vents high up in the wall would be to admit some kind of gas. Either the doctor had switched on the mechanism himself or had given some signal to do so from behind his desk. The lock on the door was an automatic one, which again could have been operated by a switch from behind the desk.

Without haste, Dr Vaucluse reached down, pulled open a drawer in his desk and took out a small portable gas-mask.

'In a very short while you will be unconscious, M'sieu Pinaud,' he said coldly. 'The gas is toxic, but not lethal.'

His voice changed and trembled with a sadistic cruelty he could not control.

'It will give me great pleasure to wait until you recover before we have a little discussion together. It will be interesting to see how much I can make you remember of what you were going to do to me.'

M. Pinaud did not answer. He heard the words but hardly troubled to listen.

Every nerve, muscle and sinew in his body was straining to get him to the door. Every last reserve of will-power in his mind was forcing them to succeed, to achieve the impossible.

He moved and swayed and staggered.

Dr Vaucluse slipped on the mask and through the mica watched him calmly with the clinical interest he probably devoted to a laboratory specimen.

M. Pinaud did not even see him. He was watching the lock on the door, forcing himself, summoning the last reserves of his great strength in one supreme effort. He could not fail now. He must not give in. He did not dare to give in. There was too much at stake. His wife was somewhere in this house, waiting for him.

The lock seemed to split sideways into parallel bands, dark and menacing against the gleaming white paint. He forced the immense weight of his gun upwards and shot at the two centre ones.

Nothing happened. His legs carried him a swaying stride nearer. Now the bands were horizontal. He shot again.

Perhaps the roaring crack of the explosion, almost deafening in that confined space, jarred his optic nerve back into focus—he did not know. Perhaps the reek of burnt cordite counteracted for a second the over-powering fumes of the gas—he could not tell. But for a brief

142

second he saw the lock clearly and emptied the magazine of his gun into it.

Chips of wood flew away around the lock but the door did not open. His eyes had seen clearly for an instant but perhaps he could no longer control his arm.

Two more staggering and yet indomitable steps and one last great effort.

With all his strength he hurled himself against the door, burst it open and fell out into the cool sweet clean air of the hall.

* * * *

For a moment he lay there on the floor, breathing deeply in great panting gasps. He did not take long to recover.

Which was just as well, because through the open door came Dr Vaucluse, tugging at his mask with one hand and flourishing a wicked-looking knife in the other.

He checked abruptly and whirled round when he saw M. Pinaud on the floor. But he was too late. One powerful hand caught his ankle in a vice-like grip and as he fell so M. Pinaud rose to his feet, treading heavily and without compunction on the hand that gripped the knife.

'There is no need for further talk, Dr Vaucluse,' he said quietly. 'Take me to my wife.'

He slid a fresh clip into his gun and stood aside. The doctor got up slowly, rubbing his hand, leaving his mask and knife on the floor.

'She is upstairs,' he said sullenly.

'Then you go first—and be quick about it. I have no time to waste.'

As they walked towards the stairs another door opened suddenly at the far end of the hall and two more men in white smocks burst in. One carried a sap in his hand, the other a tyre-lever.

Without hesitation M. Pinaud fired twice. His aim was good now that he had recovered. Both the sap and the tyre-lever thudded on to the carpet and the two men halted, each one gripping his forearm with the other hand, shock and pain contorting their features.

He motioned with his gun.

'Up in front with Dr Vaucluse,' he ordered. 'We will all go upstairs together.'

The corridor on the first floor was deserted. It ran through the central part of the house, for there were doors on either side. Each one had two strong bolts above and below the door-handle. As they walked past M. Pinaud noticed that all the bolts were closed.

Dr Vaucluse stopped outside one door.

'In here,' he said.

'Open it. Leave the door open. All of you go inside. Tell her to come out. Ask her to close the door behind her.'

They obeyed in silence.

Then she was there in front of him, and the light in her eyes was as wonderful as he had remembered it throughout the long years that had followed each other with such incomprehensible rapidity and so differently.

'I knew you would come for me,' she whispered.

He reached past her and bolted the door. Then he took her in his arms, the gun still in his hand. For a moment he could not trust his voice. The precious moment was worth all the pain and the torment and the anxiety—just to be with her again.

Then he remembered and drew back.

'Are you—are you all right? I mean—did they ill-treat you?'

'No—no—'

'Because if they did—I go in there now—'

'No. It was just like a bad dream. They gave me injections and I slept most of the time. But now it is over. Now you are here with me.'

With infinite gentleness he touched her cheeks and smoothed away the tears.

'Then there is nothing to cry about, is there?' he asked quietly.

'No—of course not—I am being silly. The shock and the reaction—'

Again he raised his hand. This time he touched her lips.

'Later—we can talk later. In the car. Just now we must hurry.'

'Yes. Of course.'

They were half-way down the corridor when she suddenly caught his arm.

'My things in the room—my suit-cases—'

Her face was contrite and woebegone, stricken with remorse.

He checked in mid-stride and turned. A sudden and radiant smile transfigured the hard strong lines of his features, reassuring her and comforting her with its irresistible charm. This was no time to be bollocking her about luggage.

'Don't look so miserable,' he told her cheerfully. 'You had better come up again with me. I can't leave you here alone. I don't know how many more of these thugs—'

'Is it dangerous?' she interrupted him quickly. 'There are three of them—'

'No—I have my gun. Come on.'

They ran back along the corridor.

'Wait outside here,' he told her. Then he drew back the bolts and opened the door, leaving it wide.

The room was simply furnished with a bed, a chest of drawers, a cupboard and a dressing-table. An adjoining door led probably to a bathroom.

Dr Vaucluse was sitting on the bed, bandaging a man's arm with what looked like the sleeve of his shirt. M. Pinaud moved his gun towards the other man, who was sitting on the one chair, still gripping his forearm.

'Quick,' he ordered. 'Those three suit-cases in the corner. Take everything off the dressing-table and put it in one of them. Then bring them to me.'

The man did not move. Dr Vaucluse stood up quickly.

'He can only use one arm and he is in pain,' he said quietly and with a strange dignity. 'I will do it.'

He swept all the toilet articles up in a bundle, using the linen cover on the dressing-table, and put them in one of the suitcases. Then he turned back the pillow, took up a nightgown and bed-jacket, reached under the bed for a pair of slippers and placed them on top. Then he closed the suitcase, carried it to the threshold and came back for the other two.

'Thank you,' said M. Pinaud.

Suddenly he felt that there was more—much more—that he ought to say. But he could not find the words. And, besides, there was no time.

He took the suitcases one at a time, still covering them all with his gun, and backed out, putting them down outside. Then he closed and bolted the door.

No one attempted to stop them as they crossed the hall and left the house by the front door.

* * * *

The found Brancard unconscious, lying face downward on the bracken in the copse, his arms flung wide.

M. Pinaud put down the two suitcases he had been carrying, one in his hand and one under the same arm, holstered his gun and dropped on one knee beside him. He passed a hand with sensitive fingers over the back of his head. There was blood on his collar and a lump at the base of his skull.

As he probed and felt, Brancard stirred and groaned. M. Pinaud grasped him by the shoulders, turned him over, partially lifted him and supported his head against his knee. The light grey eyes opened, but they were blank.

'Germaine,' said M. Pinaud over his shoulder, 'this is Brancard, from the *Sûreté,* who was supposed to have been covering me. Get back on the drive and watch the house—leave the suitcase. Yell if anyone comes out.'

At the sound of his voice Brancard moved again and his eyes focussed.

'What—what happened?' he asked.

'You tell me,' replied M. Pinaud briefly.

Brancard groaned again and put his hand up to the back of his head.

'That hurts,' he said. 'But I am all right now.'

He moved once more and tried to get up. M. Pinaud held him firmly.

'Keep still,' he ordered. 'We'll get you to a hospital—'

'Nonsense. I tell you I am all right.'

'You may have concussion. It is best to make sure. Can you remember anything?'

'Not much. Someone must have crept up behind and slugged me. I was keeping well under cover, watching the house, when suddenly there was a terrific pain and a great flash of light and I knew I was falling. I am sorry about this—I let you down.'

'No harm done,' replied M. Pinaud quickly. 'I got her out.'

'You did? Good for you.'

Then M. Pinaud placed one arm around Brancard's shoulders and the other behind his knees, lifted him bodily, still protesting, and carried him back to the car. He laid him gently across the back seat, made him comfortable and told him to shut up and keep quiet.

Then he called his wife, closed the door once she was in the front seat and went back to fetch her suitcases, which he put in the boot.

He drove away slowly and carefully, stopping twice to ask the way to the nearest hospital and to make sure that he was not being followed.

Brancard did not speak. Glancing in the mirror, M. Pinaud saw that his eyes were closed.

Once Germaine turned to him, her face eager and alight, her mouth already open, but he smiled and shook his head. He gestured with his thumb over his shoulder and whispered: 'Later.'

She nodded, caught his hand before it grasped the wheel again and pressed it to her lips.

And so in silence they brought Brancard to the Accident Ward of the hospital, where Germaine waited outside in the car while M. Pinaud's credentials and authoritative manner worked wonders with a young and helpful interne.

He told him briefly and factually what had happened, without mentioning any names or localities.

'If he has concussion,' he concluded, 'keep him in here until he is better, whatever he says. If you are satisfied that he is fit, discharge him. He can make his own way back himself, without help.'

'That is quite clear, m'sieu.'

'Now I would like to telephone—a call of some importance and privacy. May I—'

'Of course, M'sieu Pinaud,' the young doctor interrupted, indicating with his hand. 'Please use my office. Through the door. There is an independent outside line on the desk.'

M. Pinaud thanked him, walked through to the office and dialled the number of M. le Chef.

'Yes, Pinaud?'

'She is safe, m'sieu, and unharmed, thanks to your help.'

'That is wonderful news, Pinaud—I am so glad and thankful. But I did nothing—you should have all the credit.

You deserve it. How you got that name I shall never understand.'

'I will explain when I see you, m'sieu.'

'Good. You do that. Did you have any trouble?'

'Not much. Brancard got bashed on the head from behind, but I don't think it is serious. I have just left him at the Hospital of the Three Saints near the Bois de Boulogne. They are checking whether he has concussion—just as a precaution. Here is the number.'

He read off the figure at the base of the telephone.

'Thank you, Pinaud,' said M. le Chef. 'That was a good thought. What are you doing now?'

'We will call for the children at Passy and then I will take them all to Moudin. Fortunately my wife has cousins everywhere. I don't dare to take her back to the flat—not with Roche still at large—'

'Very wise. Make sure you have no tail.'

'I have done. I will again. I think, m'sieu, that you ought to send a squad to the clinic of Dr Vaucluse and charge him with kidnapping my wife and holding her there against her will. That will do for the first charge. Tell them to open all the doors which have bolts on the second floor and question all the patients who have bars on their windows. That should give you a few more charges to bring against the doctor. And tell them to check his office on the ground floor. It is fitted with vents high up on the wall to admit some gas which helps him to deal with unwelcome visitors. That should make yet another charge—unless he can explain why such equipment is necessary in a law-abiding and orderly clinic. They should have quite a day.'

'I will do that, Pinaud. When shall I see you?'

'I will either telephone or call in, m'sieu, as soon as I get back from Moudin.'

'Good. Look after yourself, Pinaud—and good luck.'

'Thank you, m'sieu. Good-bye.'

CHAPTER 7

He drew the car in to the side of the road, under the shade of a giant tree, and switched off the engine. Then he turned and took her in his arms.

Now at last they were alone together. Now at last the nightmare was over.

'Tell me all about it,' he said quietly.

She smiled in order to keep back her tears as she wondered for the hundredth time why this proud, passionate idealistic and courageous man should love her so much.

'There is not really very much to tell,' she replied. 'The driver of the hired car pulled up behind a saloon that was parked in a side-street not very far from the flat. Two men were waiting as we stopped and made me get out. One kept very close to me and showed me a knife. He said he would rather not use it but was quite prepared to do so. Then they would pretend that I had fainted and carry me to their car. There was no one about—they had chosen the place well—and so I could not do very much. He said they were going to keep me for a few days until you had been persuaded to change your mind. The other one took my suitcases and we drove out to the clinic.

'They were all polite and very correct in their behaviour. Two of the male nurses took me up to that room and then Dr Vaucluse came in and gave me an injection. And he gave me another one later in the evening. He said if I slept I would not worry so much. He was quite right.'

She paused and smiled.

'Actually—I don't think I worried at all—not much, anyway—the whole time. I knew you would come.'

Such love and trust were rare. He knew he must never cease trying to be worthy of them.

Her smile deepened.

'The things I worry about—that you drink and smoke too much and never seem to have enough time to enjoy a meal slowly and digest your food properly and eat far too much when you do and always get involved with a naked woman whenever you are investigating a case—all these things are not really important. The fact that I knew—that I never had the slightest doubt—that somehow you would find a way to come for me—that is important. And you haven't even kissed me yet—'

He did so, with humility and thankfulness.

'You are quite right. I have been far too busy.'

'What do we do now? Are we going home?'

He shook his head.

'I dare not. They know where we live. They will try again.'

'Then what?'

He thought for a moment.

'I think we ought to go straight to your parents and collect the girls. Then I take you all to Moudin—'

'To Thérèse—'

'Yes. It is a good thing you have no lack of cousins. Moudin is the back of beyond—no one will ever find you there.'

'But it will take hours—'
'That can't be helped—'
'The girls will be bored stiff—'
'I wasn't when I went—'
'That was different. We had each other. Thérèse can be trying sometimes.'
'I never noticed. The place is so lovely she just seemed to become part of it.'

He remembered his one visit to Moudin, many years ago, with nostalgia. He saw once again in his mind-sight, with vivid and poignant clarity, some of that tranquil peace and loveliness which had impressed him so much—the incredibly ancient house, kept gleaming and immaculate by willing local labour under the vigilant martinet's eye of that stern spinster Thérèse, the vast and old-world garden, bordered and bounded by a placid stream, with all its gnarled fruit-trees, its lawns and beds of thyme and lavender, the square church-tower opposite, the tall trees around the churchyard, bird-song in the morning and the darting swoop of swallows at sundown as they swept homing to their nests....

It was a forgotten corner of the world and a lovely one—too far and too remote even for Roche Enterprises.

Cheered and comforted by the thought and by his decision, he started the car and drove off to Passy.

* * * *

The small house, set neatly and tidily in its white flint enclosure, seemed strangely still and deserted.

He pressed the horn—two short notes followed by two long ones—which would normally have been the signal for the front door to be nearly torn off its hinges to allow the flying and scampering exit of his two young daughters.

But this time no one came out. The door did not open. The house still seemed to sleep, silent and deserted.

'Perhaps they have all gone out,' he said. 'Have you got your key?'

'Yes.'

'Come on, then—they may have left a note.'

They found no note, but in the small front room Germaine's father, sitting alone at the table with a bottle of brandy in front of him.

His ruddy farmer's complexion was white and strained, his eyes blank pools of memory.

'Father—what has happened—'

She took two swift steps and sank to her knees beside his chair. His eyes focussed, lit with a glad recognition, and then —dreadfully—seemed no longer to see her.

'What is it—tell me—'

He reached out a large hand as though to place it on her head, but it stayed outstretched aimlessly and pitifully, until she caught it in her own and pressed it to her lips.

Then he looked down and seemed to see her for the first time.

'They have gone—'

His voice was only a whisper, only a husk of sound like the rustle of leaves on an autumn day.

'Where? What do you mean?'

'Someone rang the bell as we were having lunch in the back room. Marie went to open the door. Two men came in with guns. They crowded her back to where we were sitting at the table, and then one of them took the girls up to pack at the point of his gun and the other covered us in the back room while we waited. When they came down the two men took the girls away. A car was waiting outside.'

M. Pinaud averted his eyes from his wife's face. The broken and tortured whisper went on, but he did not have to look at either of them.

'We have no telephone here, you know. By the time Marie had called the police from our neighbour's house and the patrol-car arrived, it was much too late. They took her back with them to the station to sign a statement—what good will that do? That is why I am sitting here alone—trying to forget.'

Suddenly, with a shocking violence, he wrenched his hand away from his daughter's clasp and grasped the brandy bottle. He refilled his glass and drank deeply.

At the mute appeal in Germaine's eyes, M. Pinaud started forward to remove the bottle, and then suddenly checked himself.

Here he could recognize so much pain and remorse and suffering that he felt perhaps it would be a merciful release if they were drowned in oblivion. And yet he wondered why these things should be. Surely none of this tragedy had been his fault. One could not expect a man of his age to argue with a gun.

The slow and dragging whisper started again to give him the explanation.

'I am a proud man. I have always had my pride. Now I feel humiliated and ashamed. I feel that I have failed both of you and myself as well.'

'In what way?' asked M. Pinaud. 'You could not possibly—'

The old man interrupted him heavily.

'These men were thugs—cheap hoodlums hired for money. In a drawer in the back room is my own Walther automatic, loaded. Thirty years ago I strangled a German officer to get it. Thirty years ago I killed better men than these swine when I was fighting with the *Maquis*—fine men—born soldiers who believed honestly that they were doing their duty—not pigs like this hired scum.

'And I did not dare to take that gun out and kill them. I thought about it— all the time that one stood there I thought about it—but I did not dare—I did not dare—'

M. Pinaud made a great effort—almost physical in its intensity—and tried to put his daughters out of his mind. His grief and sorrow and torment were for him alone—but there was an old man tearing himself to pieces and torturing his conscience with remorse for something that was not his fault.

Instead of removing the bottle he went out quickly to the kitchen and found a clean glass in the cupboard.

Then he came back, pulled up a chair and sat down at the table opposite them. He fought to control his own emotions and deliberately made his voice steady and matter-of-fact.

'May I join you in a glass? It looks like excellent brandy.'

Wordlessly the old man gestured with his hand. M. Pinaud took the bottle and poured himself a drink.

'Look,' he continued quietly, 'none of this is your fault. No one takes a chance at the wrong end of a gun. I would have had to do the same in your place, whatever I felt. I have made an enemy of this man and he is completely ruthless. But I will get them back.'

His calm acceptance of the situation and the confidence he did not feel but had forced into his voice were immediately effective against the mounting hysteria of both father and daughter. Visibly they both relaxed.

He drank the glass of brandy quickly and stood up.

Now he looked at his wife. He knew that his face had gone white, now that he was facing his own problems, but he did not know that there was a light in his eyes she had never seen before.

'Wait here for me,' he told her gently. 'I don't know how long I may be—but wait here for me.'

He paused at the door.

'Make your father some black coffee,' he added. 'And when Marie gets home, all three of you should have something to eat. It will help to pass the time.'

And then he was gone.

* * * *

He got into his car and drove like a madman through the city, risking his own life and that of others not once but many times.

And all the time he drove his thoughts easily outpaced his car. And this time they were neither about engine revolutions nor strain. Roche was clever and efficient enough to have two strings to his bow—an alternative plan ready made to counter what had happened at the clinic—but how could he have known that the children were at Passy? When Germaine had taken them in a taxi two days ago he was not even on the case.

And then, cutting across the front of a bus with centimetres to spare, he remembered what Germaine had told him about Dr Vaucluse and his injections. If one had been of scopomaline she would not remember telling him where they were.

He pulled up and parked in a side-street behind the enormous building and ran quickly up the shallow steps past the black marble sign.

He traversed the vast entrance hall rapidly and yet without any outward appearance of haste.

At the desk the blonde receptionist recognized him and opened her mouth to speak. By that time he was already pressing the button of the first automatic lift.

'It is all right,' he called out briefly over his shoulder. 'M'sieu Roche is expecting me—I telephoned him at home.'

The doors slid open smoothly and he was gone before she could speak. All the way up to the fifteenth floor he was wondering whether she would telephone to announce him. It would not affect the issue, but it might cause complication. In any case, it was too late now to do anything about it.

The doors opened again and he stepped out. He remembered the door of Madame Arnaud's office and the red-haired secretary remembered him with a glad and lustful smile, which he ignored.

'M'sieu Roche's office, please,' he said hardly. 'He is waiting for me. As quickly as you can—we are both in a hurry.'

Janice Arnaud lost her smile at the tone of his voice as quickly as she had found it and pointed wordlessly, her eyes wide and frightened, to the inner door at the far end of her office.

This M. Lebrun, who had been so

charming, so virile and so irresistible that very same morning, appeared to have changed, and not for the better. There was a look in his eyes, my dear—she recounted to her girl-friend that evening—which made me feel positively ill. Of course—I did not argue. But I was glad that his business was with M'sieu Roche and not with me.

'Thank you,' he said, walked quickly across the room, and opened the door without knocking.

****

From behind a large desk in the beautifully furnished room Roche looked up from a low armchair in surprise.

For a moment no one spoke. M. Pinaud shut the door quietly behind him with one hand. With the other he aimed his gun steadily at Roche's head.

'You look surprised, M'sieu Roche,' he said. His voice was quiet, and yet there was a menace in it which caused the other man to sit very still.

'I am,' he replied. 'I heard that you had found your wife. But on the other hand—'

'You have my children,' the quiet and deadly voice interrupted him. 'We will come back to them in a moment. First of all, you will telephone the switchboard operator and tell her you are not accepting any calls and that you are not to be disturbed here until you let her know.'

'You must be mad—to think that you can get away—'

'Now.'

Again M. Pinaud interrupted him.

'Do it now—or else I will kill you with as little remorse as I would tread on vermin.'

Roche reached for the telephone at his side and gave the instructions correctly. M. Pinaud holstered his gun. Then he walked over to the desk.

Roche replaced the receiver. Without haste he reached across the desk and lifted the lid of a large and beautifully chased silver cigarette box which stood in front of his tooled leather blotting-pad.

His hand was inside when M. Pinaud moved with incredible speed. In one bound he covered the last two steps to the desk and slammed the lid of the box down hard on the hand and the small automatic it was actually grasping.

Roche moaned with pain and the blood drained from his features, leaving them deathly white.

For a few seconds M. Pinaud kept the pressure on the lid, then he released it. Roche snatched his hand away and held it to his mouth, which continued to make small moaning noises behind it.

'You have been playing rough,' M. Pinaud said then, still in that same quiet and menacing voice, as if nothing had happened. 'I am going to teach you how others can do the same.'

Deliberately, he moved around behind Roche and suddenly pushed the armchair close to the desk. He set one foot and leg firmly against its back. With one hand he spun his gun over, one finger in the trig-ger-guard, and held it by the barrel. With the other he grasped Roche's left hand and slammed it down flat on the polished mahogany beside the blotting-pad, hold-ing the wrist in a grip like a vice.

Roche struggled futilely. He was powerless against M. Pinaud's strength. The chair, with its arms encompassing him, seemed welded to the floor.

The gun lifted and the butt crashed down on the nail and tip of Roche's forefinger. The noises he made now were almost inhuman.

'You have more fingers, M'sieu Roche,' M. Pinaud told him, his voice completely devoid of any emotion. 'Where are my daughters?'

Roche writhed in agony, but did not answer. Only those animal sounds still bubbled from his drooling and trembling lips.

'You are fortunate I have my wife back,' M. Pinaud continued, 'otherwise I think I would have killed you. As it is, I am quite prepared to kill you now—slowly. Where are they?'

He raised the gun again.

'No—no—no more—'

The resonant voice was no longer recognizable. It was a strangled gasp. Roche's nerve had broken.

'Where are they?'

The question was still without emotion. But it was also ruthless and pitiless and terrifying in its intent.

'In my house.'

'At St Germain?'

'Yes.'

M. Pinaud released his grip, spun the gun again until he held the butt and then stepped back from the armchair.

'You will come with me to fetch them,' he said. 'Where is your cloakroom?'

Roche staggered to his feet and gestured towards a door at the far side of the room.

'Wrap a small towel around your hand and keep it in your pocket. And at the same time get your hat.'

Roche hesitated.

'Go on, then. I shall be behind you, every step you take. If you have a bar in this room, take a shot of brandy—that will steady you. Tell Madame Arnaud and the telephone operator on your way down that you are going out with me, but that you will not be long. And remember that I will be covering you all the time. I have every justification for putting a bullet in your back and no compunction at all about doing it.'

* * * *

They left the building together without incident. Obviously none of his employees ever questioned or argued with Roche.

Outside M. Pinaud hailed a taxi. He could not control Roche and drive his car at the same time. As the driver pulled in to the kerb, he waited, a pace behind Roche, until he stepped forward and gave the address in St Germain des Près.

Once inside, he settled back in his corner, one hand still in his pocket.

'Your friend, Dr Vaucluse,' he said, 'will be arrested and charged with kidnapping, which is a serious offence. There may even be other charges as well. This is easy. Your case and proving your complicity will be more difficult. There is no proof that you ordered him to do it except my word. There are no witnesses. Your money can buy the best lawyers and even judges as well.'

He paused, but Roche did not answer.

'I prefer therefore to leave you free— I know now where you live and where you work—so that I can come back myself and kill you if ever you dare to interfere with my family again.'

Still Roche did not answer. They sat in silence until the taxi-driver drew up outside the house.

After that scene of violence in Roche's office the actual return of his children seemed to M. Pinaud—as so often after moments of tension and strain—to be almost an anticlimax, hardly believable in its detachment.

They did not even enter the house. He stood behind Roche in the porch with his hand still in his pocket, while the other man rang the bell and opened the front door with his key.

To the man who appeared Roche spoke briefly.

'Fetch M'sieu Pinaud's children down at once, please, with their suitcases.'

'Very good, m'sieu.'

This must be the secretary Brancard saw, he reflected. Roche waited in the porch. Very soon he stood aside and then they came out, each carrying a small suitcase.

'Hullo, Pa.'

'Hullo, Pa.'

It had to be anticlimax, because this was not the time for emotion.

'I am glad to see you both,' he said quietly, and if his voice was a little unsteady as he made the understatement of the year, no one seemed to notice.

'The taxi is waiting—in you go.'

Once they had passed him, swinging their suitcases, jumping and clattering down the steps, he moved the hand in his pocket slightly forward.

'Inside,' he told Roche, 'and shut the door.'

The door slammed. He turned and ran quickly down the steps to the taxi.

During the short drive to Roche's office building to pick up his car he had time to ask them and to reassure himself that they had not been harmed or ill-treated.

But the whole of the somewhat longer drive out to Passy was completely dominated by fervent and almost unending ejaculations of wonder and praise for the super record-player which they found when once they had been locked up into what was actually a small and practically self-contained flat under the roof of the house.

'Pa—you never saw anything like it—'

'Four loud-speakers—'

'F.M. amplifier—'

'Quadraphone, that creep told us—'

'The sound just curled round the back of your ears, Pa—'

'And seeped into the sides of your brain—'

'What a stylo that must have been—'

'Helical cuts and all that—'

'Why can't we have one like—'

'Stupid—it must cost thousands—'

He sighed philosophically at the gulf—more, the immeasurable abyss—that seemed to sunder the modern offspring from their parents, refrained from comment and contented himself with watching the rear-view mirror to make sure that no one was following them.

And so he brought them back safely to Germaine and her parents in the small house at Passy, from which, after a brief rest, he set out on the long journey to Moudin.

CHAPTER 8

Now once more he was at home. Now he was at peace.

His family were safe in Moudin. He had ensured, not once but many times, that no one was following them. As a final precaution, since he knew that part of the Massif Central well, he had turned off the road just before dusk, switched off his lights and waited, in spite of his impatience, for a quarter of an hour in the shadow of an old barn.

He waited and watched and let the traffic go by until he was quite sure. Then he took the next side road and came into Moudin down a lane that apart from the local inhabitants very few people knew.

He refused all offers of hospitality from Thérèse, and after a quick cup of coffee drove back to the city.

Now he could relax. To him that meant a drink and a packet of cigarettes, and consequently the small room was soon thick with acrid blue smoke, the coffee-pot empty and the level of the second bottle of brandy diminished by an astonishing amount.

He felt the peace of the moment rise up within him like a warm sun, melting and dispersing the cold dank mists of tension and strain and anxiety that had swirled about him all that day.

Another man, justifiably, might have felt proud. But not him. He knew only humility and thankfulness. He knew that he had been helped. He knew that his prayers—when eventually the night before he had found the words—had been answered. In that recognition there could be no room for pride, only gratitude.

This mood of blessed relaxation did not last—could not last for long with one of his nature. He began to think of Roche and what Roche would do next and what he himself ought to do before he did it.

Then he went into the hall and telephoned M. le Chef at his home.

'Yes, Pinaud?'

'I am really sorry to disturb you at this time, m'sieu, but I was too late to call at the office. I have only just returned from Moudin.'

'So you took them there as you had decided.'

'Yes—but only after some delay.'

'Why was that?'

'When we got to Passy the children were not there. Two of Roche's men had taken them away at gun-point.'

'Incredible—what happened then? I presume you got them back, since you went to Moudin—but how?'

'I went straight to see Roche in his office, m'sieu, and persuaded him to tell me where they had been taken. Then I went with him to fetch them from his house in St Germain.'

His voice was devoid of emotion. He might have been reading a report. There was a long silence. He waited patiently until it was broken.

'I think it would be advisable, Pinaud, if I tell you now and make it quite clear that I did not hear any of your last remarks. There is probably a fault on the line. We can resume this discussion in the morning at the office.'

'As you wish, m'sieu. I shall be there early. There is one more thing—'

'Yes?'

'I think I should go to Gothenburg tomorrow.'

'What on earth for?'

'To try to find out more about that barge. I know it is important but I cannot see how. If you remember, m'sieu, Henri Rostand had a letter from Spanlo, the marine engineers, and he also flew there, according to his wife. I would like to know why he had to do that. Would you get someone to book me a seat on the morning plane so that—'

'It sounds like a wild-goose chase to me, Pinaud.'

'It is the only clue we have, m'sieu.'

'I suppose you are right. You are usually right, Pinaud, about things like this.'

'I know, m'sieu. The trouble is—'

'That is what makes you so infuriating,' the decisive voice interrupted him for the second time. 'But no matter. It might be a good idea. Just hold on a moment while I look at my engagements.'

Obediently M. Pinaud waited. It was a long moment.

'In that case we will postpone our discussion until the morning after. You can get there and back in a day. I have an idea that the first plane leaves Orly fairly early. You had better go straight there—get on the telephone yourself now, find out the time and book your seat. It is not too late. And don't forget the one coming back. I want you here in the office early in the morning after. It fits in better this way—Brancard will be here then. They are letting him out tomorrow afternoon and he is going straight to Mitterand to do his shift watching the warehouse. There was no concussion.'

'Good—I am glad to hear that. And thank you very much, m'sieu. I will get on the telephone to Orly now.'

'Right, Pinaud. See you the day after tomorrow. Good luck. Good-bye for now.'

'Thank you, m'sieu. Good-bye.'

* * * *

He remained in the hall and dialled the

SAS office at Orly Airport to book his flight. The first plane was full and the only return available was in the early afternoon. He would not have much time in Gothenburg. As he replaced the receiver, the doorbell rang.

He walked very slowly and without making a sound down the corridor, grasped the handle and then suddenly tore open the door so that the first thing the caller would see was the gun in his hand.

It was Victor Marvin. He stood there on the doormat, nervously twisting his hat-brim with both hands, his faded blue eyes blinking apologetically.

'I am so sorry to disturb you at this—' he began.

M. Pinaud stepped back and holstered his gun.

'Not at all,' he interrupted cheerfully. 'Please come in, M'sieu Marvin—and forgive this somewhat rude reception. I was expecting a different kind of visitor.'

'Thank you—this is very kind of you. I am not intruding, I hope—'

'Of course not. I am alone. The family are away. Come in here and sit down.

Will you join me in a fresh pot of coffee?'

'Well—gladly—if it is not troubling you—'

'No trouble. I was just about to make another one for myself. Make yourself comfortable—here—take the armchair. I shall only be five minutes.'

When he returned he poured the coffee and a glass of brandy for his guest, which gave him an excuse to pour another one for himself, as a matter of normal social courtesy. Then he leaned back in his chair.

'Now then, M'sieu Marvin,' he said quietly, 'what brings you here?'

The slight figure stiffened in the depths of the capacious armchair. He seemed even more frail and disconsolate than when they had last met.

He began to speak at once, slowly and hesitantly at first, and then, perhaps reacting to M. Pinaud's sympathetic silence, with rapidly increasing fervour and confidence.

'I know you will forgive my presumption, M'sieu Pinaud. Your kindness and sympathy yesterday gave me the courage

182

to come here. I looked up your address in the telephone book. I had to talk to someone. I am so worried about Yvette. She is not getting any better. Sometimes I wonder if she will ever get better. She still refuses to tell me anything. She will not confide in me. As I told you yesterday, we have become strangers. But since I have known that you are investigating this case, I feel a new confidence. I feel that at last there is hope. I have heard a good deal about you, M'sieu Pinaud, and I have even read about some of your exploits. If anyone can find Henri's murderer, it will be you. And then I am sure she will start to mend.'

He paused and drank some brandy. Then he leaned forward in the chair.

'M'sieu Pinaud, I have a favour to ask you.'

'And what is that?'

He kept his voice carefully non-committal. Surely he had enough on his mind at the moment without getting involved in anything else.

'I would like to help you in your investigations—no—wait—'

As M. Pinaud swiftly opened his

mouth, Marvin held up his hand in a gesture that was strangely dignified and somehow infinitely pathetic.

'I know you probably think that I am a silly old fool, but she means so much to me and it could just be that I might prove of use. I am prepared to do anything— if only it can help her—run errands, take messages—anything that would perhaps make it a little easier for you. I would do whatever—'

The eager voice died as M. Pinaud stood up.

'M'sieu Marvin,' he said slowly. 'I would like to feel that you have no doubts about the sympathy I have for you and your daughter. But what you ask is quite impossible, and even if I agreed, would never be allowed by our regulations. My investigations must not be divulged to anyone and have to be carried out by myself alone. On the occasions I need help, I have already been provided officially with an able and experienced assistant. I am very sorry to have to disappoint you, but this is a favour I am unable to grant.'

His voice was kind but firm and final.

Marvin seemed to shrink in his chair. His disappointment was obvious and made words unnecessary. M. Pinaud poured him another brandy and then continued:

'On the other hand, if you would give me your address and telephone number, I promise that I will keep you informed if I make any progress.'

Marvin stood up and drank his brandy.

'That is very kind of you,' he said quietly. 'Here is my card—I am not far from Yvette. And now I must go—I have taken enough of your time. I thank you once again, M'sieu Pinaud, for your courtesy and kindness.'

And then he went out, a small and tragic figure strangely ennobled with the dignity of his great and unselfish love....

* * * *

Of the beautiful city of Gothenburg M. Pinaud saw nothing.

He would dearly have liked to have spent some time in its harbour, visiting the Elfsborg fortress and the celebrated Götaplatsen.

But immediately he descended the

gangway from the plane at the airport, he hurried to the nearest telephone. There, with the aid of an operator who was not only multi-lingual but also intelligent, he succeeded in making an appointment with Dr Runnström, the managing director of Spanlo AB.

Dr Runnström, his secretary said, would be pleased to see him if he did not waste time in getting to the factory from the airport, since the morning had been a busy one.

In a few moments, therefore, he was sitting in a large diesel-engined taxi, with his back to the harbour, the fortress and the Götaplatsen, which he would so dearly have liked to see, and driving at a furious speed out to a plain vast enough to dwarf even the gigantic buildings which had been erected thereon.

Dr Runnström received him courteously in his office on the ground floor, waved away his credentials and immediately won his heart with his opening remarks, uttered in fluent and faultless French.

'I am delighted to meet you, M'sieu Pinaud. You must not think that because

186

we live so far away we are completely ignorant. Thanks to Thomas Förlag, we are familiar with some of your more famous exploits. It is both a pleasure and a rare privilege to meet you in the flesh. Please take a chair—good.'

Dr Runnström was tall, large and powerfully built. He also radiated an intense and infectious energy. Instead of a jacket, he wore an immaculately tailored three-quarter-length linen coat, whose whiteness a surgeon might have envied.

In many ways he reminded M. Pinaud of a Swiss banker he had once met during one of his earlier cases.

Both held themselves with that supreme and innate self-confidence which comes naturally to a man when a trade, or craft or some technical skill has been thoroughly and competently mastered. Both had close-cut hair. Both had features which seemed carved as hard as granite by the lines of austerity and self-imposed discipline inherent in years of study. And both wore white linen shirts, starched and laundered to an almost incredible degree of immaculate perfection.

Dr Runnström waited until he was

comfortably installed in the armchair and then sat down himself behind the desk.

'Now then—what can I do for you?'

'First of all,' replied M. Pinaud, 'let me thank you most sincerely, Dr Runnström, for your welcome and your courtesy. Together, they make my work so much easier and more pleasant.'

He sat forward in the chair and his voice changed.

'Now—my reason for seeing you is this. We have reason to suspect a certain man in Paris of planning to run a cargo of heroin down the river to one of the main ports. There is a barge involved, at present empty, which we are keeping under surveillance. Recently, a man named Henri Rostand, who was employed by our suspect, received a letter from you and then came here to see you. I have a strong suspicion that this barge was concerned—'

'You are quite right, M'sieu Pinaud,' Dr Runnström interrupted. 'Just one moment.'

He pulled out one of the lower drawers of his desk, bent down in his chair to read names, and then pulled out a manila file, which he opened and placed on the desk in front of him.

'Roche Enterprises in Paris,' he continued. 'We had the first letter from them some weeks ago enquiring whether we could supply and install a special engine in a barge. We replied with our normal letter assuring them that we were willing and able to co-operate. We are always receiving such letters. The majority of our clients, we have found, once we have talked to them, invariably agree with us in the end that their ideas of special are fully satisfied by one of our standard engines.

'In their reply they elaborated their requirement. It was for a unit that would enable the barge to make a very fast trip to the coast with a full load. The cost was immaterial and would be paid by return. Banker's references were enclosed.'

He looked up at M. Pinaud over the width of his desk and a very slight softening, which might have been the beginning of a smile, touched the strong mouth for a fleeting second.

'I did not waste time writing letters to

enquire what they meant by very fast. Nor did I waste more time in listing my thoughts and speculations. I assumed—deliberately, since I am paid to make a profit—that it was a matter of cargo priority and a desire to outpace their competitors. I had no suspicion that they might wish to outrun a police-launch. In any case, the river is too well patrolled for any barge to do that, whatever the engine. And the thought never occurred to me that there was anything questionable enough in their request to warrant a visit from the *Sûreté.*'

'What did you do, then?' asked M. Pinaud.

'I telephoned instead, suggesting that they send someone over here to discuss the matter with me, as there might be certain technical problems involved. Which they did. One Henri Rostand, as you said. He is one of the senior accountants in—'

'He was, Dr Runnström,' interrupted M. Pinaud quietly. 'He is dead. He was shot in the back of the head, his body weighted and thrown in the river. We have reason to believe that he was murdered near the wharf beside which the barge in question is moored. That is why I am here.'

Dr Runnström looked grave.

'I am sorry,' he said quietly. After a short silence he glanced down again at the open file.

'Do you wish me to go on?' he asked.

'If you please.'

'One of the problems was that here we do not believe in altering or modifying in any way our existing engines. Each model we manufacture embodies the results of years of intensive research and experimental design, meticulous planning, exhaustive tests and an astronomical sum of money invested in expensive machine-tools. On the other hand, we also do not believe in losing orders—as I said, we are here in business to make a profit. The welfare and happiness of some five thousand families depend on my decisions. The client was obviously prepared to pay well and quickly for a special order.'

'Who signed the letter?' M. Pinaud interposed quickly.

For a long moment Dr Runnström

looked at him in silence. Then he shook his head slowly, as if in reproof.

'Come now, M'sieu Pinaud—this is a confidential business file. Its contents are therefore private. I would not show it to you or answer your question unless you could produce a signed letter of authorization from your superiors. And even then I might argue—once with you and once again in a court of law if you brought me there. Our business relationships with all our clients are strictly confidential. They have to be. Besides—'

Here he paused and a charming smile completely transfigured his granite features.

'Besides—you already know the answer to your own question—or else you would not be here.'

M. Pinaud smiled too. He liked this man and admired him for what he was, quite apart from the fact that his shrewd assumption was quite correct. He did know.

'Shall I continue?'

'Please.'

'There is not very much more information I can give you. I suggested to

M'sieu Rostand, therefore, that in view of the problems involved, we should install two—not one—of our high-power marine engines into the barge. There was enough space to make this feasible—he had the forethought to bring the specifications with him—and by linking the two engines together with one of our own patents, a special selective and automatic coupling, so that either or both could be engaged as required, the necessary power and speed would be available.

'He agreed to my suggestion and confirmation of the order was sent. I dispatched the engines about two weeks ago — on the seventh I think—yes—with a team from the factory to install them.

'We did this while the barge was moored at the quay. There were certain conditions to the order. They were in a hurry and did not want the barge moved. If they had allowed us to ship the barge here, the installation would have been child's play. In that case we would naturally have fitted twin drive-shafts and twin screws.

'Since the barge had to remain in the water, this was not practical. The single screw had to stay. This gave us problems, I admit. I had to spend hours on the telephone with our foreman.'

He paused, and once more the hard lines about his mouth softened in a smile.

'But believe me, M'sieu Pinaud—and I am sure you have found this out for yourself—there is no problem that cannot be solved if one is prepared to think about it long and intelligently enough. And perhaps I should add that provided the client is prepared to pay at a very high rate for each hour of thought then there can be no better inspiration. All the problems were solved.'

He closed the file with an air of finality. M. Pinaud took the hint and stood up.

'Thank you, Dr Runnström,' he said. 'You have been most helpful. So far the barge has been riding high and is obviously still empty. We did not think to examine the engines—although even if we had we could not have done very much until it was loaded. But this barge is obviously the key to the whole operation—we must watch it very carefully. Thank you once again. I will not detain you any longer.'

Dr Runnström stood up as well and glanced at his watch.

'It was a pleasure,' he said courteously. 'If I have been of any use I am glad. I must leave you now, as I have another appointment—but would you care to take a walk through the factory?'

M. Pinaud hesitated and was lost.

'One of my foremen can speak French,' Dr Runnström continued. 'Half the fun is asking questions—he will be able to answer most of them. He pulled a ligament in his shoulder, argued with his doctor and came back too early, but as we will not allow him to work, he has nothing to do.'

He pressed a button on his desk and held out his hand.

* * * *

And so, accompanied by a gigantic young Swede, he spent the next two hours in a state of ecstatic enjoyment.

He saw the furnaces and molten metal being poured. He saw more presses, drills, punches and automatic high-speed lathes than he had ever seen assembled together before in his life.

He saw men who were highly paid and who not only took a great easily recognizable pride in their work but also seemed to enjoy it, obviously thankful and grateful for the intelligence that had planned so meticulously and so methodically to make it interesting.

He walked with forgings and castings and pressings and turnings until they finally became marine engines, keeping up an incessant stream of questions, the majority of which the young foreman managed to answer.

When the tour came to an end he was thoroughly exhausted but extremely happy. He thanked his guide the foreman with sincerity and decided not to offer him a tip, since his monthly salary was almost certainly far greater than his own. He understood now why these engines held a reputation that was worldwide.

The taxi had to be driven at an even greater speed to catch his plane, and so he finally left the city of Gothenburg without even having seen the magnificent harbour, the Elfsborg fortress or the famous Aveyn leading to the celebrated Götaplatsen.

CHAPTER 9

The two chairs were no longer in front of M. le Chef's desk.

The courtesy of Brancard's introduction having been duly fulfilled, protocol was now firmly re-established, and they both stood repectfully on the magnificent Aubusson carpet, made fully aware by their very position that there was only one authority in that beautiful room, whose status gave him the privilege of sitting behind the carved ormolu desk, giving orders to all those whose lack of privilege and status condemned them to stand in front of it.

'Before you begin to tell us about Gothenburg, Pinaud,' the voice of authority began without preamble, 'there is one point on which I would like a little more information, if only to clarify the thoughts in my mind. I had the impression last night—I cannot be sure because there was interference on the line—that you mentioned something about having persuaded Roche—'

M. Pinaud opened his mouth to speak, but a wave of M. le Chef's hand effectively silenced him.

'No—wait. Let me finish. Conrad Roche is a man with the power and the money to make it very awkward for us here should he decide to do so. Have you given him any justification?'

'Yes, m'sieu—ample. But you need not worry. He will not do anything.'

'Why not? How do you know?'

'Because the last thing he wants at this juncture—in the middle of whatever scheme he is concocting—is publicity. And besides, he knows that he would have no case. He had my children kidnapped. I have witnesses. I persuaded him to tell me where they were. He agreed. It was his idea to play rough. I showed him how. That is all there is to it.'

Brancard, whose hair had been shaved to allow the taping of a large pad of gauze to the back of his skull, did not say anything, but he looked at M. Pinaud with a very thoughtful expression in his eyes. M. le Chef considered for a long moment and then allowed a very faint smile to touch his lips.

'Very well, Pinaud. Now tell us about Gothenburg. What did you learn?'

'Enough to confirm that the barge is important, m'sieu, and I am sure is going to be used. Roche had new engines fitted by Spanlo to make it capable of a very fast run to the coast and sent Henri Rostand to the factory to discuss their installation.'

M. le Chef nodded thoughtfully.

'I see,'

'With your permission, m'sieu,' said Brancard. 'This is a method of which we have had experience in Marseilles. The heroin is taken by boat to a port along the coast, sunk at night outside the harbour in waterproof containers marked by a buoy, and then picked up almost immediately for shipment to America. There is always some port official amenable, provided the bribe is great enough.'

He paused and hesitated.

'Go on, Brancard,' said M. le Chef.

'M. Pinaud here has told us that it is a

sugar warehouse at Mitterand. This again is a method we know. All the granulated and demerara will be genuine and opened on demand; the heroin will be in identical packets amongst the caster-sugar. There need not be a great bulk to represent a fortune.'

'Very interesting,' said M. le Chef. 'That is why we have been keeping a watch on that warehouse ever since Pinaud had his trouble there. You did your shift yourself last night, did you not, Brancard?'

'Yes, m'sieu. I got back from the hospital in the afternoon, went to bed, and took over from midnight to six, as we agreed on the telephone. But—'

Again he paused and hesitated.

'But what?'

'I know that was the only building available, m'sieu, where we could get concealment—but the view from those windows is mainly of the warehouse. You can barely see the barge.'

'I know that. We assumed that the barge would be loaded from the warehouse, since that has been involved from the beginning. It was there that Pinaud was ambushed.'

'Yes, m'sieu—but that does not necessarily follow,' put in M. Pinaud quietly. 'The cargo could have been transhipped from another barge or boat, especially at night.'

'Yes,' agreed Brancard, quickly and eagerly. 'He is right. With your permission, m'sieu, I think we ought to go there and check at once.'

There was a moment of silence, while M. le Chef looked from one to the other, Brancard eager and tense, M. Pinaud thoughtful and composed. Then his look changed to one of doubt.

'I agree—but should you not take a squad—'

It was M. Pinaud who shook his head decidedly, thereby successfully interrupting him without actually committing the unpardonable offence.

'No, m'sieu. Roche has his spies and watchers everywhere, as I know well.'

'With the siren going full blast on the van,' put in Brancard, 'they would be gone and the heroin hidden by the time we got there.'

'All right,' agreed M. le Chef reasonably and quietly. 'I see your point—no squad. But these are desperate and unscrupulous men—and we do not know how many there will be against the two of you. Let me arrange to get you some more detectives in private cars—'

Brancard, as a newcomer, obviously did not know about the unwritten and yet none the less scrupulously observed and rigorously enforced law prohibiting, under any circumstances, the interrupting of M. le Chef while he was speaking.

He therefore transgressed unwittingly, but nevertheless definitely and effectively, since M. Pinaud noticed that his eagerness had now given birth to both impatience and excitement.

'Yes, m'sieu—thank you for your offer—but this is a matter of great urgency. It is vital we go there at once. The cargo could be on board now. If we delay talking any more here the barge may be gone when we get there. What I mean is—can you produce them at once?'

M. le Chef eyed him with what M. Pinaud recognized as a singular tolerance, which he knew full well that had he himself been the transgressor he would never have enjoyed.

'No, Brancard—I cannot. That is asking for the impossible. Contrary to popular opinion, perhaps fostered by imaginative television scriptwriters, I do not have a private waiting-room in this building where my detectives sit and wait for crimes to be committed. I would naturally have to contact them on the radio-telephone and if possible detach them from what they are doing since, as you mention, the matter is urgent. The first two or even three, may well find this impossible and therefore some delay is inevitable. However—yes, Pinaud, what is it?'

M. Pinaud had opened his mouth halfway through this speech and deliberately kept it open. Over the years he had found that this was another quite effective method of gaining the great man's attention.

'With respect, m'sieu—and with great appreciation of your offer—I would venture to suggest that Brancard is quite right. We have no time to wait now.'

'Very well,' agreed M. le Chef. 'Are you sure you can manage on your own?'

'Of course, m'sieu,' replied M. Pinaud. Brancard was already half-way to the door. 'Provided he does not get himself bashed on the head again.'

****

They drove to Mitterand in M. Pinaud's car quickly and efficiently and—since all the *Sûreté* cars have private number-plates—unobtrusively.

There was hardly any conversation. Brancard did not speak. M. Pinaud wondered about this, and then decided that perhaps the blow on the head might still be affecting him. Or he might even have taken the joke about it the wrong way, as a personal affront.

He therefore maintained a sympathetic silence, concentrated on his driving, and in a remarkably short time pulled up on the cobblestones in front of the warehouse.

The place appeared to be empty. As they got out of the car and walked up to the quay they both saw that the huge sliding-doors were open but that the interior of the building seemed deserted.

On the other hand, as they came to the quay, M. Pinaud noticed that the barge was now laden with cargo and deep in the water. He also saw that it was ready to cast off. Only one mooring-rope, from the stern behind the wheelhouse, was still attached to a bollard on the quay.

Even as they approached, a man climbed out of the hold in front of the wheelhouse and walked towards the rope, with the clear intention of casting off.

The river was bleak and bare and almost deserted. The early-morning barge traffic had long since passed and it was still too soon for the normal flow of traffic.

Brancard spoke to him. His face was eager and taut, his gun in his hand.

'You take him,' he said. 'I'll go to the wheelhouse—there might be one or two more in there.'

For a moment M. Pinaud felt like arguing and putting him, with a few well-chosen phrases, in his proper place. After all, it seemed a little hard when a complete stranger—a newcomer, a transfer from what might well have been a minor post in Marseilles—presumed to open his big mouth in this way and dictate a course of action to the eminent Pinaud, who, whatever his failings and his limitations, could yet claim with justifiable pride of having had twenty of his more famous cases authentically published.

This was supposed to be a team, M. le Chef had said, in which Brancard, who had been transferred in order to assist, would do what the captain—which every team must have—told him to do, and not a partnership in which Brancard, brandishing his gun like a television detective, gave the orders to implement the strategy he himself had formulated.

And yet—and yet—with that quick and instinctive insight which always enabled him to sympathize with the other point of view, he realized exactly why Brancard was on edge and aggressive in this way and so eager to prove himself. On the last occasion they had collaborated together at the clinic of Dr Vaucluse, he had hardly distinguished himself. And he might well have held an important position in Marseilles—and therefore would be all the more eager to prove himself and justify his appointment in the eyes of M. le Chef.

He smiled faintly to himself and decided not to make an issue of the matter.

'All right,' he replied. 'Take care.'

They slid down the ladder quickly, Brancard in front. The man was kneeling beside the rope and did not even look up as Brancard passed him on the way to the wheelhouse.

'Tighten it up again,' M. Pinaud told him quietly, motioning with his gun. 'We will not be leaving yet.'

The man took no notice of him either, called him two words that were rude even for a bargee and loosened another coil.

M. Pinaud thought swiftly. The report of a shot might distract Brancard, should he be having trouble in the wheelhouse. The fact that the man had ignored them seemed to indicate that a trap or an ambush, with reinforcements in the hold, might well be waiting there for him. Far better to keep it quiet.

He took two quick steps forward, spun his gun around with his finger in the trigger-guard, grasped the barrel firmly and hit the man hard on the head.

He took two quick turns on the mooring-rope to tighten it up again and then moved back, gun once more ready in his hand, to the sprawling and unconscious figure.

As he jerked the handcuffs out of his hip-pocket and bent on one knee to fasten one-handed the limp wrists together behind the man's back, he was conscious of a vague and yet definite unease.

He felt that there was something wrong, but he could not determine what it was. Still on one knee, having snapped the handcuffs shut, he looked towards the wheelhouse. The door was still closed. He should never have let Brancard go in there alone. If two of them had been inside waiting for him, ready for the second the door opened, Brancard would not have had a chance. And yet—he should have heard something. And if that had happened, surely they would have been out by now to deal with him. There was also something strange about the way this man had come out only to cast off—

At this precise second his introspection was suddenly and painfully interrupted as a heavy boot kicked his elbow from behind with such savage violence that it sent his gun flying over the side into the river.

His reactions brought him to his feet like a cat. One forearm and hand were jarred and throbbing and momentarily useless with the force of the kick; the other hand as he came up was closed in a vice-like grip around the man's ankle.

The two of them must have crept silently down the ladder from the quay while his back was turned. Both held long and wicked looking knives in one hand.

He tightened his grip on the ankle and with one quick and tremendous heave hurled the body into the path of the second man who was actually rushing at him, crashing them both together in a heap of flailing arms and legs.

One outstretched hand on the deck still grasped a knife. Without a second's hesitation he stamped on the wrist and heard the bones crack. But before he could turn and stoop to snatch up the knife the man had reached out to grasp it with his other hand. With the toe of his heavy boot he kicked the hand and saw the knife curve over the low deck into the river.

Then the other one was on him, the knife stabbing low in a practised hand with the thumb held upwards. He stepped forward instead of back, felt but ignored a cold stab of pain as the blade gashed his forearm, and stepping close and inside caught the man's wrist with both hands, forcing his slashed arm to take part of the strain in spite of the agony of the effort.

He dropped to his knees in the same movement and still gripping the wrist, hurled the whole body over his shoulder to crash down head first on the wooden planking of the deck.

The knife dropped from the nerveless fingers. The first man was quick, but M. Pinaud was even quicker. One foot came down hard on the blade, dark with his own blood, and before he straightened up, the other drew back and then swept low across his body in a deadly *savate* kick that caught the man full in the lower stomach.

Then he collapsed exhausted on the deck, his wounded arm doubled up against his chest beneath him, while the water and the sky swam and merged and mingled in front of his eyes in one great grey and threatening wave.

Even as his body fought to regain breath after that superhuman effort, so his mind struggled as desperately to retain consciousness, in order that he could answer the questions he knew were waiting somewhere behind that sombre and terrifying wave in front of him—why had Brancard stayed in the wheelhouse—why had he not come out to help?

* * * *

When Brancard eventually came out, he was still carrying the gun in his hand. Only now it was fitted with a silencer.

One swift glance took in the bodies of the three unconscious men and the figure of M. Pinaud lying awkwardly face-downwards on his doubled-up arm with the gouts of blood darkening the planking beside him but he did not pause. The pale grey eyes were intent and, remote, seeming to look far beyond what they saw.

He walked straight to the engine hatches by the stern and opened both covers. Then he knelt down and put his free hand inside. M. Pinaud heard the starters whirr and in a moment the twin diesels burst into life with a throaty roar and then clattered evenly together.

He only had that moment, while one of the open hatch covers hid him from view and while Brancard was occupied with the engines, but he did not waste it.

The knife he had trodden on was close beside him, on the side of his wounded arm, almost concealed by the leg of the man he had kicked.

He did not hesitate. Ignoring the pain, in one supreme effort that made his senses reel, he forced his body up a fraction, reached out with his wounded arm to grasp it and pulled it back under him. It would not be of much use against a gun, but it was the only weapon he had, and while there was life in him he would go on fighting, even without a weapon, even with only one good arm....

Brancard straightened up, but he did not return to the wheelhouse. He took the few steps quickly to the stern and began to uncoil the last mooring-rope. Then he ran lightly up the ladder, cast off the mooring-rope from the bollard and flung it down on to the deck.

Then M. Pinaud knew.

Before, even the speculation of suspicion would have been monstrous, unheard-of, incredible. Now, the isolated thoughts in his mind seemed to settle into place by themselves, without his volition, forming a design, completing a pattern.

Brancard slid down the ladder and walked back to the wheelhouse. He opened the door wide, moved the throttles forward and stood in the entrance, one hand on the wheel. The note of the diesels deepened in a surge of power and the barge glided smoothly and effortlessly out into midstream.

After a moment Brancard slipped the rigid clamp over one of the wheel-spokes and walked back towards him.

M. Pinaud tensed but did not move. He watched him through half-open eyes. The river was clear until the next bend.

But Brancard did not come near him. Keeping to the far side of the two unconscious men, his silenced gun still in one hand, he stooped and with the other grasped each one in turn by the ankle, dragged them across the deck with a powerful heave and slid them over the side. Then he did the same to the man M. Pinaud had handcuffed.

Unhurriedly, he walked back to the wheelhouse, freed the wheel and stood there once again in the entrance, one hand steering the barge, the other still holding his gun and his eyes glancing back continually at M. Pinaud in unceasing vigilance.

* * * *

And then M. Pinaud began to speak to him.

He spoke carefully and unemotionally, not loudly but clearly to pitch his voice above the clatter of the diesel engines, and not hurriedly, but with a deliberation that was successfully compelling.

He spoke because he was so helpless that there was nothing else he could do, and as he took each isolated thought out from that particular place in the pattern into which it had flown he was gratified to see how this dissection only confirmed and strengthened the meaning of its destination.

'I can understand now how this barge could be loaded unobserved during a twenty-four hour watch. If you were paid enough to look the other way during your shift, there is no mystery. And I see now why you were so eager to get me on board this morning. Dead men tell no tales is an old saying—but I am not dead yet. Until you have killed me it can have no meaning.'

Brancard did not answer. He moved his hand so that the gun was concealed between his body and the open door and continued to steer the barge out and away from the bank downstream.

'You were in the office,' M. Pinaud continued, without any change in the inflection of his voice, 'when I mentioned that my children were at Passy. To trace the house was not difficult, but Roche could only have known they were there through you.

'And now I can see why I had to get my wife out of that clinic alone. You never thought I would—after you had warned Dr Vaucluse. That was why he was ready for me with his gas—that was why so many male nurses kept on appearing. And that was why you did not get concussion. Did you know it is rare with a self-inflicted wound? There is an instinctive aversion to striking hard enough to induce it.'

Still Brancard did not answer. M. Pinaud thought with even greater intensity. He must not give up. He could not afford to give up. In his helpless condition that was the only chance he had. He must try to provoke him, to goad him, to get him to move a little nearer—just a little nearer from the wheelhouse.

So now as he spoke again his voice was no longer emotionless but became cruel and insulting with a scornful and vindictive contempt.

'How much did Roche have to pay you to forget the oath you once took and betray your employers? Your experience in Marseilles with his filthy drug traffic must have doubled the price. But perhaps he got you cheap—perhaps you just enjoy your work. After all—kidnapping children—'

'Shut up,' suddenly yelled Brancard. 'You talk too much.'

M. Pinaud obeyed. The order had come too late. There was no need to say any more. He had achieved his object. The words he said, with all their implications, were now in the man's mind. He only had to wait. He only had to lie there, without moving, and try to retain enough strength in his burning and throbbing arm so that it would not fail him.

It was Brancard who spoke first. His voice was once again controlled and cold with menace.

'Later on, as soon as it begins to get dark, you are going the same way as Henri Rostand. And I will take more care with the weights than those fools did with him.'

'That may be,' M. Pinaud replied. 'But do you realize that you are wasting your time? By now the Chief will have the alert out—this barge will be held at the port or even at the next—'

'Why should he?' Brancard interrupted. 'Why should he do anything? He may wonder why we have not telephoned, but why should he worry or take action? There are two of us—and surely two of his detectives should have no difficulty in handling a barge crew—especially if one of them is the famous and celebrated Pinaud.

'And by dawn this cargo will be out at sea on the morning tide. This was all organized, down to the last detail, weeks ago—long before you came poking your impudent nose into what does not concern you.'

Abruptly his voice changed.

'Now get down into the hold—out of sight. The traffic will soon be building up and I don't want anyone to see you lying like a crippled dog on the deck.'

M. Pinaud stiffened, made a great and obvious effort to raise himself and then collapsed with a loud and realistic groan.

'I can't,' he said weakly. 'I can't move. I think they must have broken my arm.'

'Then I shall have to drag you,' Brancard told him.

He turned and clamped the spoke of the wheel once again. In a few seconds he would leave the wheelhouse and walk back along the deck towards him.

This was his chance, he thought. These few seconds comprised the only one he would get. Flung into the hold he would never be able to climb out unnoticed with a wounded arm.

Now, he told himself—now. Whatever the pain—now.

He forced himself up on his wounded arm. His good hand groped and found the knife under him. His fingers closed around the hilt, quickly and yet lightly delicately, sensitively—feeling and estimating the weight and balance. Then his fingers clenched.

In spite of the exruciating pain he put yet more weight on the other hand, forcing his failing strength into one last great effort, lifting his body even higher until his good hand and the knife were clear

Brancard came out of the wheelhouse backwards, because his first concern was to make sure that the way ahead was clear for the barge.

Then he turned, saw M. Pinaud and the gun whipped up in his hand.

But it was too late.

With all his remaining strength and

kill M. Pinaud had already hurled the knife.

He aimed deliberately high, for the shoulder of the hand that held the gun. This man was too important to be killed at that moment. This man's evidence would be vital, whatever his conviction later—not only in presenting the case against Roche but also in cleaning up some of the corruption in Marseilles.

But at the very last instant—a fraction of a second before the knife left his hand —his knee slipped in a gout of his own blood and his arched body jerked forwards and downwards.

For another fraction of a second he saw the light gleam on the blade like a darting metallic thread, and then there was only the hilt protruding like some obscene and pointing finger from the centre of Brancard's stomach.

* * * *

There was nothing he could do. The man was dead before he hit the deck.

M. Pinaud felt no remorse. Brancard would have killed him without compunc-

tion. He had lost a witness, but saved hi
own life. This was not the first man h
had killed, but always their deaths ha
been in self-defence. And this one ha
been an accident: he had meant to woun
and not to kill.

He felt no remorse—but because of hi
very nature he could not escape regret
The very solemnity and the awful finalit
of death always saddened and humble
him. Even as he forced himself int
action he remembered the words of Joh
Donne—any man's death diminishes m
—and those words in their awesom
majesty seemed to resound and rever
berate inside his head as he staggered t
the wheelhouse and pulled the throttle
back to reduce the speed of the barge.

Then he removed the clamp, spun th
wheel over hard and steered the barge'
bows straight into the nearest bank.

Next he switched off the engines an
with some difficulty and more pain extri
cated himself from his jacket. With hi
penknife he cut off the sleeve of his shir
at the shoulder, split the cloth lengthwis
and with his other hand and his teet
managed to bind a temporary bandag

around his wounded arm. The knot he
tightened with the silencer of Brancard's
gun into an improvised tourniquet.

Which reminded him that he would
have to draw another gun as soon as he
got back. M. le Chef would need this one
—a standard issue illegally fitted with a
silencer—as evidence against Brancard at
the inquiry that would surely be held in
Marseilles.

Then he sat down philosophically on
one side of the engine hatches and waited
for the next patrolling police-launch.

CHAPTER 10

The enormous doorman, glittering and resplendent in his magnificent uniform, eyed him contemptuously, recognized him and turned his back ostentatiously. For him, such individuals did not exist.

The receptionist sagged in horror and visibly wilted inside his uniform, until it appeared that only the stiffness of the massive gold braid sustained him from collapsing.

Even the imposing liftman's eyes protruded like organ-stops as he removed his hand from the double bank of complicated buttons and asked his passenger, in a voice filled with incredulity and dismay, to repeat his instructions.

By this time it was borne upon M. Pinaud that his recent activities on the barge had done little to improve the appearance of his suit, and that cutting the sleeve off a shirt, regardless of the exorbitant price his wife had paid for it as a present for his birthday, hardly aided the fit of that garment across his powerful chest. If one also took into consideration the odd splashings and stains of his own dried blood, both from his wound and the knife on which he had lain, he reflected moodily, it was hardly surprising that the aspect he presented was not a prepossessing one.

In a voice as cold as the North Pole and as hard as iron, he repeated his instructions to the liftman, brandished his badge under the man's nose, inflated his chest under his unbuttoned jacket so that his new gun was visible in its shoulder-holster, and then waited silently until the gates swung open noiselessly on the fourth floor.

That is three of them, his sardonic reflections ran on, who have looked at me as though I was something the dog had done. All I need now is the balding Victor Marvin to materialize like a phantom from out of the low ceiling, confront me and look at me in the same way as the others and then forbid me emphatically to go near his lovely and beloved daughter. Surely there must be an easier way for a man to earn an honest living.

But neither ghost nor phantom nor even flesh-and-blood father appeared as he walked on towards the flat.

His heavy boots trod slowly and silently on the rich and yielding pile that carpeted the seemingly endless corridor, but his thoughts raced backwards with fantastic speed in a continuous cycle of vivid and almost frightening clarity.

When the inspector on the police-launch had taken him back to Mitterand and finally decided—after requesting his signature on an unbelievable number of official forms—that he might be permitted to return and report to his office, M. le Chef had been stupefied, triumphant, elated, jubilant, enthusiastic and concerned. In that order.

Stupefied at the fact of Brancard's betrayal and defection; triumphant, elated, jubilant and enthusiastic at the thought of the capture of several million francs' worth of heroin by the *Sûreté,* and finally concerned at M. Pinaud's appearance and wound.

He had argued, begged and pleaded that a doctor be summoned forthwith.

He had advised and recommended an immediate blood-transfusion in the nearest hospital. He had praised and congratulated his most famous detective and done everything except kiss him;

When he finally realized that M. Pinaud—dirty, exhausted, bruised and wounded—was determined neither to rest nor give up, he had pushed himself out of his chair, crossed over the room to an inlaid marquetry sideboard which had once graced a drawing room in Versailles, and poured out with astonishing liberality an enormous balloon goblet of the most exquisite brandy M. Pinaud had ever tasted—which did him far more good than all his words of advice.

With great reluctance he refused another, for he knew that his stomach was empty and the diabolical strength and flavour of that incredible spirit still seemed to surge up from his intestines to his brain and back again in a stream of molten fire whose incandescence compelled an apprehension that almost completely obliterated all his appreciation....

Then be begged to be excused and took a taxi to the Sixteenth Arrondissement, since he had found it an arduous, painful and exhausting task to drive his car practically one-handed from the warehouse to the Quai d'Orsay.

* * * *

Now he rang the bell of Number eight. Again he had to wait a long time before the door opened.

She wore a loosely-belted housecoat with a gay floral pattern. It was obvious that she had nothing on underneath.

Her manner was apathetic and dull. She looked at him without interest. She made no comment on his appearance, which he found in welcome contrast to the attitude of her landlord's minions. Her eyes seemed more concerned with trying to see through him and beyond him.

'Pinaud from the *Sûreté,* madame,' he said quietly. 'Do you remember me?'

In spite of her lethargy, he saw that the sapphire-blue eyes were astounded, wide with astonishment. The hesitation, the pause, confirmed his suspicion into a certainty. She had never expected to see him again. This was why he had refused to finish M. le Chef's exquisite brandy. This was the reason why he had forced himself to come here, instead of going to a doctor or a hospital.

She made a great effort to control herself.

'Of course I remember you,' she said. 'Do come in.'

She held the door wide open.

'Please forgive my bad manners, but it is getting late and I go to bed early.'

As she turned to hold the door in its new position, the two folds of the house-coat swung free and parted beneath the loosely-belted sash. M. Pinaud found that he had considerable difficulty in keeping his mind concentrated on the purpose of his visit, which now, suddenly and inexplicably, seemed to have shrunk to complete insignificance....

Nevertheless, his conscience compelled him to do his duty.

'Madame Rostand,' he said, as soon as she had ushered him into the living room and the same luxurious settee. 'I have just one question to ask you.'

Now his voice, deliberately, was hard

and stern and official.

'The last time I saw you here, to bring you news of your husband's death, you made a point of telling me that the warehouse on the quay at Mitterand, where almost certainly he was murdered, belonged to one of Roche's companies. May I ask why?'

She had sat down in an armchair opposite him, decorously drawing the housecoat together. Now she crossed her legs and ignored the folds as they fell aside once more. She looked at him frankly and if she sensed that his eyes were not meeting hers, she gave no sign.

'Of course. I thought that this information might help you in your investigations.'

'Is that all? Was there no other reason?'

'I don't know what you mean.'

'I think you do, madame. After what you told me about his objections to one of Roche's schemes it was perfectly obvious and logical to assume that I would seek the connection and go there.'

His eyes shifted up from her housecoat and watched her closely.

'Now this is the interesting part, Madame Rostand. Until an hour before I saw you, I was not even assigned to the case. After I left you I went straight to Mitterand.'

There was no point in telling her about his conversation with her father. She might even know already. In any case, it would make no difference.

'No one knew I was going there,' he continued. 'No one could possibly have known. And yet two men were waiting for me when I arrived—two men who tried to kill me. How could they have known I was coming? How could Roche —who gave them their orders—have known—unless someone told him? Your whole conversation, madame—everything you told me about your husband the last time I was here—was deliberately planned with one purpose, to make me call at that warehouse. Did you tell him, madame—as soon as I had left you?'

* * * *

At least he had broken through her apathy. She looked at him for a long moment, thoughtfully and appraisingly, and this time her eyes saw him. Then she rose gracefully from her chair.

'Would you excuse me for a moment, M'sieu Pinaud,' she said. 'It is time for my medicine.'

She had done this before. He thought of following her unexpectedly and then decided against it.

He waited without moving until she came back, the same flush on the high cheekbones, the vivid and lovely eyes even more brilliantly blue than before.

Then, without speaking, he got up and walked slowly over to her chair. With one swift and sudden movement he grasped her wrist, pulled up the loose sleeve of her housecoat and revealed the numerous puncture marks on the inside of her arm.

She stiffened and recoiled. He allowed the loose sleeve to drop back.

'This is not my business, Madame Rostand,' he said quietly, 'but may I remind you that you have not yet answered my question.'

She did not reply. The silence seemed to surge up from the floor like some great and all-encompassing wave, parting them, dividing them, sundering them to remain for ever apart....

Deliberately he changed the tone of his voice.

'I have a prison-van waiting downstairs, madame. The women's prison at La Santé is a rough place you will not enjoy. And there are no facilities inside for your medicine. I have a warrant in my pocket for your arrest on a charge of accessary to premeditated murder. Since you refuse to answer my question here, would you kindly get your clothes on so that I can continue your questioning there.'

His voice was cold and merciless. He lied swiftly and smoothly, fluently and effortlessly, without any scruples of conscience. This woman was somehow tied up with Roche, who smuggled heroin to make a profit and who had kidnapped his wife and daughters. This woman could supply him with the evidence he needed. One method had failed. He was prepared to try any other.

She stared at him in horror. The words poured out, quick and eager and terrified.

'I don't know anything. I don't know what has been happening. I have not been to work, not since—'

Abruptly she stopped.

'Not since your husband's disappearance?'

Now his voice was gentle and kind, but she did not answer.

Then he had one of those rare flashes of intuition whose almost uncanny insight largely accounted for his eminence. He remembered that she had told him she was one of Roche's personal secretaries. He remembered the red-haired Madame Arnaud in her adjoining office, who also was another. And from what he had seen of Roche, there were almost certainly more.

'Not since Conrad Roche told you he had finished with you?'

There was another silence—somehow horrifying—between them. Then the tears came, healing and merciful, and she buried her face in her hands.

* * * *

M. Pinaud let her cry. He sat bolt upright on the massive settee, took out his packet of cigarettes and lit one.

This would do her good. These were the tears she should have shed long before. Perhaps some of them were for her dead husband. He hoped they were.

Half-way through his first cigarette he noticed that there was no ash-try in sight. Without compunction he allowed his ash to fall on the expensive carpet and trod it in unobtrusively. This was a moment no one should dare to interrupt. This was a silence sanctified by sorrow and remorse, grief and regret. A bill for cleaning an expensive carpet, whatever the amount, would not even begin to turn the scales of the balance.

He dropped the stub of his cigarette, ground it again into the pile with his boot and lit another.

Still he waited, with infinite patience, until at last she lowered her hands and raised her head.

'What—what do you want to know?'

'Everything, madame. I suggest you begin at the beginning.'

She began to speak, but he held up his hand.

'Wait—before you start, may I say one thing. I would like to help you. One can have treatment—'

She stared at him incredulously. This could not be the same man. His voice was now rich and warm and understanding, and gentle with an infinite kindness and compassion.

She shook her head violently.

'No—no—it is too late—'

'It is never too late,' he interrupted, gently and yet with a conviction that caught and held her interest. 'There is no future for you in going on like this. There are clinics—'

Again she shook her head as she interrupted him with a laugh that held nothing of mirth, only bitterness and scorn.

'Clinics? Like the one of Dr Vaucluse? Have you been there? Did you see those —those things—they are no longer human beings—he keeps behind bolts and bars in those upper rooms? Would you have ever believed—'

'I have been there.'

He interrupted her deliberately to quell the mounting hysteria in her voice. His face had gone white at the memory.

'Roche kidnapped my wife and Dr Vaucluse kept her there. I went to get her out—but I had not time to see anyone else.'

'Just as well. Conrad told me that heroin would be fun—that the stimulation would made a dream of our lovemaking. Imagine—a multi-millionaire who wanted to sleep with his secretary—and a young girl who knew nothing—who had no experience of the world—who believed every word he said. I did not have a chance. He gave me a car—money—clothes—everything I wanted. He said he loved me. Like a fool I believed him. Far better to have believed my father—but he always told me everything in the wrong way.'

Again the tears came, dimming the brilliant blue lustre of her eyes. This time for a moment she allowed them to brim over, splash and fall unheeded, without moving her hands, which made her suddenly, poignantly as pathetic and as vulnerable as a child.

M. Pinaud waited. He had that rare gift of silence which was more sympathetic than any words at a time like this. Now the dam was broken. Now he only had to wait. Now the relief of telling him —the very words themselves—were providing the anodyne she so desperately needed.

'Before all that happened I had met Henri Rostand. He was so good and so kind. He was the kindest man I have ever met. I was restless and unfulfilled—I thought marriage would be the answer. The difference in our ages would not be important. I told you our marriage was a failure. So it was. But it was only a failure after I became Conrad's mistress and he started me on drugs. Then it never had a chance.

'Conrad is a man who is completely evil. I can see that now—when it is too late. He has no conscience, no scruples, and cares for nothing except money. I see now that he deliberately set out to seduce me as soon as Henri began to thwart his plans. Henri objected to this scheme of shipping heroin, which was so important to Conrad and represented so much profit that he was prepared to do anything—even murder—to get his own way.'

She took a handkerchief from the pocket of her housecoat and wiped her eyes.

'I make no excuses,' she continued quietly. 'I helped him with my eyes open. If I must face the consequences, I accept them. I must have been mad—mad with infatuation. I did everything he told me to do. I believed everything he said. During all that time he continued to say he loved me and would take me away with him on a cruise as soon as this deal had been completed. I believed him and I obeyed him. With him I had no pride. He made no comment when I told him that Henri had disappeared—but if I had been sane and in my right mind and not taking these filthy drugs I should have known. He would not have cared if I had —he is that sort of man. Even after that I still had to do what he said. He threatened to order Dr Vaucluse to cut off my supply unless I kept him informed.'

M. Pinaud found it increasingly hard to sit there in silence. Compassion, disgust and a white-hot anger seemed suddenly, all together, to be tearing him to

239

pieces. And yet he forced himself to sit there and listen, sickened by what that quiet and hopeless voice was telling him, knowing that words were useless, praying in all sincerity that in her confession this unhappy and ill-used woman might find some measure of mercy and peace....

* * * *

'I betrayed you, M'sieu Pinaud,' the quiet and tragic voice continued, sad now with an infinite longing and regret. 'I betrayed you the first day we met. I telephoned Conrad as soon as I heard you were coming. He told me to tell you about the barge at Mitterand. He knew you would go there and gave orders for you to be killed.'

She paused for a moment and then looked at him directly.

'Does that answer your question, M'sieu Pinaud?'

'Yes,' he replied immediately. 'You need not worry any more about the prison-van. Now that you have told me the truth, you have nothing to fear.'

She considered for a moment and then seemed to make up her mind.

'In that case—' she began, and then suddenly stopped.

'In that case—what?' he prompted her gently.

Again she looked directly at him, but this time he was sure that the blue eyes did not see him.

'In that case,' she repeated slowly, 'perhaps you had better go now. There is nothing that you can do.'

He waited for a while, as if considering what she had said, and then he leaned forward and spoke to her in a voice whose intensity of kindness and compassion she had never heard before.

'You are wrong, Madame Rostand—entirely and completely wrong. There is a great deal that I can do—and am willing and anxious to do it. I can find you a good doctor. There are clinics—not like the one you know—where you can be cured. Let me—'

She shook her head hopelessly and interrupted him.

'It is too late—'

'No,' he burst out violently. 'It is never

too late. That is nonsense. That is cowardice and defeatism. You must look forward, not back.'

Again she shook her head.

'You are trying to help me, M'sieu Pinaud— I can see that. I am grateful. But you are wasting your time. It is of no use.'

'But—'

She held up one hand in a gesture that had a strange dignity.

'No. Just go now. I am tired. You can come to see me in the morning, if you still want to.'

He stood up at once and she smiled.

He realized that it was the first time he had ever seen her smile. It was a lovely smile and yet not a happy one. He seemed to see in it a wistful yearning for all that might have been, and a tragic acceptance of the futility of her desire. Behind it and in it he caught a glimpse— breathtaking in its radiance—of that wonderful beauty which once had been hers.

'All my life,' she said to him quietly as he turned to go out, 'I have tried to find happiness—perhaps because I was so

happy as a child with my father. When I
found it—I realized I had found nothing.
Only fools and lunatics keep on looking.
Good-bye, M'sieu Pinaud. Thank you
for trying to help me.'

He had faced her to listen. Now he
turned again towards the door. It was
obvious that she wanted to be alone.

CHAPTER 11

He walked slowly down the long corridor, in his memory her last words—with all their poignancy, their sadness and their terrifying realism—resounding and repeating, over and over again, in an endless and pitiful refrain.

Twice he stopped and turned and hesitated, convinced that he should go back, and each time he reasoned with himself, logically and calmly and dispassionately, as he had been taught and trained to do for so many years.

Look, Pinaud, he told himself severely, she has had a hard time, and you made it worse by being rough with her. You had to do it. This is your job. So it is no use blaming yourself. She is a drug-addict. And she has had to endure the mental strain and humiliation of being that swine's discarded mistress. She is probably, for the first time, now feeling remorse for her husband's murder. She has enough thoughts and memories to keep her awake for a year—listening to you and your good advice will never help her to sort them out. She said she was tired. She asked you to go. She told you to come back in the morning. Perhaps the drugs make her sleep—she may feel better then.

All this is true, he reflected after he had finished castigating himself with such commendable severity, and as a factual summary is really not a bad effort. What, then, is still worrying you? Why are you standing here with your hand outstretched towards the lift-button and making no attempt to press it?

Something she said. Something—no— not in the actual words themselves—but in the way she said them. There was some meaning there I should have recognized —something I should know. Something I did recognize at the time—but which I don't know now—something—

He shrugged and gave it up. He was tired—exhausted both physically and mentally. It had been a hard day. He would see her in the morning and sort it all out. They would both feel better then.

He sighed and pressed the lift-button.

The lift-gates swung apart soundlessly. M. Pinaud lit a cigarette.

'Down, please,' he said briefly.

The liftman carefully averted his eyes and pressed the appropriate button. Before they reached the ground floor, a red light suddenly flashed in a separate panel above his complex row of controls and a klaxon filled the interior of the lift with a deafening and nerve-shattering clamour.

'What on earth—' began M. Pinaud.

'Emergency alarm,' the liftman answered briefly as the gates swung open on the ground floor. His voice was perfectly polite and non-committal, but the look in his eyes left no doubt as to whom he considered responsible.

* * * *

Gold Braid was not at his desk. From the switchboard a bell was ringing stridently and uselessly, because no one was there to answer it.

Nor was the doorman in his doorway.

Wondering, M. Pinaud walked through the entrance—hall and out between the open front doors.

The block of flats, as befitted its dignity and the amount of its rent, was well illuminated with flood-lights.

He saw them both at once, the doorman and the switchboard operator, bending over something in the courtyard which ran parallel to the narrow street flanking the north side of the building.

As he came nearer, he knew.

He threw away his cigarette and lengthened his stride. He felt impelled to go, although already he knew. There was no need even to look any more; in the glare of the floodlights he had recognized at once the gay floral pattern on her housecoat.

'What happened?' he asked quietly.

The doorman was in the process of removing his fantastic coat and did not answer. The switchboard operator looked up and recognized him at once.

'Suicide, m'sieu—from the balcony of the fourth floor.

'Why do you have to tell him?' growled the doorman. 'We are waiting for the police. There is no need or obligation to talk to anyone.'

'I am the police,' M. Pinaud told him quietly.

The doorman obviously did not believe him.

'Police—oh yes—likely—with that suit and that shirt—'

He was expecting an immaculate inspector in a gleaming new patrol-car and his ideals had been shattered. M. Pinaud hardly fulfilled his expectations. Surprisingly, it was Gold Braid himself who spoke up on his behalf.

'Truly,' he said, 'this one is of the police. I have seen his credentials myself.'

The doorman grunted in derision, folded his magnificently resplendent coat neatly with some difficulty and placed it reverently on the low stone wall.

'May I—may I look at her?' M. Pinaud asked gently.

Both men looked at him curiously, for there were tears in his eyes, but made no move to stop him as he bent lower and nearer.

Miraculously, her face was hardly disfigured. He was comforted to see that there was peace and tranquillity and no

248

distortion or agony, on the strangely composed features. It was as if she had shut her eyes in anticipation of the long and peaceful sleep, so that the brief nightmare of that hideous plunge she could ignore in the belief of the blessed repose and ease as its end....

And he was thankful that he could recognize now in death far more of that glorious beauty which had once been hers than her tragic life had ever revealed.

Then, suddenly, he understood what had been puzzling him on the way back along the corridor, and because of his nature he felt both remorse and guilt.

Good-bye, she had said, and not good night. She had asked him to come in the morning, knowing well that by then it would be too late. Her decision must already have been taken. Had she expected to see him, it would have been good night. And she had thanked him for trying to help, with a sweet sincerity that should have alerted him, thus fulfilling her last obligations and saving herself the trouble of writing a note if those thanks were important enough to her to need expression.

But it was too late now for both remorse and guilt. Life and death wait for no one, and regret for what has already happened is the most futile of all emotions.

'What are you doing with that coat, Jules?' Gold Braid asked the doorman in a loud voice.

'I am going to remove her. She is bleeding all over my flints.'

'You know very well you are not allowed to do that, Jules,' Gold Braid told him in a patient voice. 'Nothing must be moved or touched until the arrival of the police. I have already put through the call. They will be here any moment. Even M'sieu Pinaud here, you must admit, neither touched nor moved. He only looked.'

Jules grunted again, picked up his coat as if it were made of Dresden china, and began to put it on. Since this operation required the facility of a contortionist, the muscles of a blacksmith and the agility of a baboon, the process—even for one of his physique—was a lengthy one.

'Besides,' continued Gold Braid, with perhaps the slightest trace of sarcasm in his voice, 'these new scientific police will probably want to determine the angle of curvature of the fall, the acceleration of the mass per second per second, the kilogramme or tonne force per square centimetre of the impact—and a number of other equally vital facts. To achieve all this successfully measurements have to be taken and recorded before the body is moved.'

M. Pinaud forgave him the sarcasm, whose overtones were apparent even above the unending sequence of grunts from Jules as he persisted manfully with his dressing. After all, the doorman Jules was probably his friend, and if a sufficient quantity of blood soaked into those immaculate white flints the task of cleaning up would not be an easy one.

And then, like vultures swooping out of the nothingness of a cloudless sky, the usual idle crowd of gaping spectators materialized from nowhere—all curious, all sympathetic, all profoundly and ghoulishly interested, all overflowing with good advice, all talking at once and not bothering to listen, all fascinated by death and all completely heartless and useless.

'Just look at her, the poor thing—'

'Let us hope, at least, that someone has had the intelligence to call the police—'

'I would say call the builders—these modern windows are not safe—'

'That is true—tear all the windows out and sue the landlord—'

'Bloated bloodsuckers—'

'No—no—the ambulance. She may still be alive—'

'Nonsense—from the position the fall indicates a great height—'

'And from the blood—'

'I tell you my aunt Rosalie knew a man whom the police carted off straight to the morgue, where he sat up and—'

'Those three types around her are talking and jabbering like apes and doing nothing. She may be dying even now—'

'Dying in agony—the poor thing—'

'Perhaps the large one will have the decency to cover her with his coat—'

'He is putting it on, not taking it off—'

'Near the Bastille one hears this is a

daily event—'

'But this is the Sixteenth—surely when one pays through the nose for the neighbourhood—'

'Someone must have driven her to do such a thing—'

'She looks so young and beautiful—poor unhappy one—'

'Men are such pigs and swine—'

'My uncle in St Onésime le Flumenières—'

'My cousin in Oran—'

'Threw him off the top floor, broke his neck, and he got up and walked away—'

'Murderers—beasts—assassins—'

'Last Sunday we were right under the jet which fell out of the sky—'

'I read about that—one hundred and eighty-five dead—they were all in small pieces—'

'We were going out on a picnic anyway with the children—'

'We found this little wood nearby and we were able to watch all the time we were eating—'

'Those three men can't possibly be the police—'

'Then what are they doing there with her—'

'Actors probably—two of them are wearing fancy dress uniforms—'

'And the other looks like a rag-and-bone man—'

'All living together in the same flat, I bet—'

'Scandalous—'

'This is what goes on today—'

'Drunken orgies—'

'Perverted parties—'

'Sexual deviations—'

'May even have pushed her out—'

'Men are such swine—'

'Why are there no police here to arrest them—'

'For this incompetence we pay rates—'

M. Pinaud pushed through them and past them, profoundly thankful to see the two patrol-cars that just then glided to a halt by the kerb.

Although there were limits to human patience and endurance, he felt it would not have been fitting to have added to the violence already unleashed in that select and decorous neighbourhood of the Sixteenth Arrondissement.

* * * *

He felt a hand on his arm, turned swiftly and saw Victor Marvin beside him.

His features were shocked and ravaged by grief, the pale blue eyes swimming with tears.

'You know?' M. Pinaud asked quietly, his voice both gentle and kind.

'I recognized the housecoat. I gave it to her as a wedding-present.'

M. Pinaud waited. He forgot the moving people, he saw nothing of the massive block of flats. He heard no sound. For a moment he did not know and cared less where he was.

He just waited, alone with this unhappy man in his sorrow, the two of them isolated in a world of their own, hoping that his silence and his sympathetic understanding might be of some use, perhaps even of some comfort.

Marvin spoke again.

'She is dead—of course—'

'Yes—I am afraid so. It was quick and merciful. She could not have felt any pain.'

'What will they do with her?'

'I should imagine they will take her to the nearest precinct station for the moment, until they notify you officially. Would you care to go with them now, M'sieu Marvin—I can easily arrange it with one of the—'

'No—no—I could not stand that. The last time we met we quarrelled. The memory would be riding between us. That is my bitterness now—now that it is too late—'

His voice suddenly choked and stopped, and again in spite of all the noise and movement and activity all around them—M. Pinaud felt the slow sad surge of the tragic silence in that world where the two of them waited alone.

He continued to stand there. What this one needs, he reflected sombrely, remembering vividly the last time they had emptied the carafes of Anjou together, is a good strong drink. He wants to talk. He has a compulsion to tell me again all about it—what he has already told me once—why not? If talking will help him, then I can help him by listening.

'M'sieu Marvin,' he began gently, 'You have had a terrible shock. At a time like this a little alcohol can be a great comfort. Would you care to come with—'

And for the second time the older man interrupted him, this time without vehemence, but eagerly and excitedly.

'Yes, M'sieu Pinaud—you are quite right in what you say—but you have already done far more than your share. You have been so kind and generous on the last two occasions we have met—this time I must insist that you come back with me. I live quite near here—ten minutes' walk. And besides, I would like to talk to you about—about this. We shall be quieter and more comfortable in my flat.'

M. Pinaud agreed readily and thanked him politely. They began to walk towards the main road, but almost immediately Marvin stopped.

'Forgive me, M'sieu Pinaud—but may I hold on to your arm?'

'Of course.'

'This—this thing has upset me—more than I thought—thank you. Thank you very much.'

* * * *

The flat was roomy and spacious, the top half of an old-fashioned house.

Marvin opened the front door with his key, ushered him in and led the way upstairs to a lofty room furnished in impeccable taste with a few really beautiful pieces of period furniture.

'Please sit down, M'sieu Pinaud,' he said, gesturing towards one of the two comfortable chairs drawn up to the oval mahogany table. 'I shall not be long.'

'Thank you.'

These were the first words Marvin had uttered since they began to walk together away from the scene of the tragedy. M. Pinaud had made no attempt to talk. If ever a man needed silence, it was this one holding his arm. He had been guided and directed by the pressures of the hand on his arm, and as they turned into the drive the latchkey in the man's other hand had obviated the need to ask questions.

Now Marvin switched on a set of wall-lights and came back from the sideboard

258

carrying a bottle and two glasses. It was a litre-sized bottle of clear glass, almost full with a liquid of a remarkable green colour.

'This is a liqueur distilled from plums,' Marvin told him. 'A farmer friend of mine makes a little every year and always presents me with a bottle each time I visit him.'

He placed the bottle and glasses on the table and sat down in the other chair beside M. Pinaud.

'I always keep it,' he went on, 'For a very special—'

Suddenly his voice died. His features seemed to crumple like melted wax and he covered his face with both hands, bowed his head on the table and cried like a child, with all the awful abandon of a child's desolation, to whom grief is the end of the world.

M. Pinaud neither spoke nor made a sound.

His thoughts were confused and chaotic. He moved his body slightly in the chair, to place the bottle and glasses out of harm's way, and noticed that each wall-light seemed to reflect a different shade of green through the bottle with every movement he made.

Then he thought that whatever worldly triumphs or successes people achieved in a lifetime, their total worth paled into insignificance beside the number and the sincerity of the tears that were shed at their death....

He reached out a powerful and muscular hand and placed it, with a gentleness infinite in its compassion, on the thin and bowed shoulder beside him.

Still he did not speak. Still he would not intrude.

The green of an emerald, he thought, and at the same time the green of a cornfield in spring. The green of jade and the green of a dragonfly's wing. All the greens in the world seemed to be imprisoned inside that bottle. He would move again later and see if he could recognize some more.

* * * *

Marvin lifted his head and lowered his hands.

'Forgive me,' he said quietly.

M. Pinaud withdrew his hand. He had left it there—for comfort, for reassurance, for sympathy and understanding—until now his arm was numb from the shoulder down.

He took the bottle and made a big production of pouring and filling the two glasses. He had given of himself, unreservedly, wholeheartedly, generously, as was his way, and now he felt like a priest after confession, like a surgeon after a lengthy and complicated operation—drained of vitality, empty and exhausted. Besides, this would give him the time his voice needed to become steady.

'There is nothing to forgive, M'sieu Marvin. There can be no disgrace in tears —only pride. Your daughter may even be able to see them—who knows—and then she will honour you for them.'

There was a long silence, Marvin did not answer. But slowly, almost imperceptibly, he began to straighten in his chair.

'Here,' M. Pinaud continued, lighting a cigarette. 'Drink this. It will do you good.'

'Thank you,' he whispered and drank slowly.

M. Pinaud drank as well, but he swallowed deeply. Then he gasped—when perhaps another man might have choked —in joy and ecstasy and even perhaps, at first, in unbelief. To make sure, since the logical mind never accepts anything without proof, he drank again and finished the contents of the glass.

Then he had no more unbelief. This was incredible, but it was also true, because he believed it. This was the father and mother of all liqueurs. This made even the brandy of M. le Chef resemble mother's milk. This was impossible—and yet it had happened.

Without daring to speak he grasped the bottle, refilled his glass and drank again, this time slowly and solemnly— even reverently.

It was like a liquid fire—encased in a cool sweet silk glove—which eased it down into the pit of his stomach and then gently and deliciously—dying and melting and evaporating the very substance of its being as it did so—manipulated it up back again into his brain, where he knew the glove was no more, no longer existed, leaving nothing but the fire and the stimulation and the excitement, which all flowed together down again to his stomach—and with it and under it and in it and through it always the sweet sharp crisp tang of the plums, as exquisitely positive as if he had actually been eating them off the tree....

He drank again, moved the bottle—which gave him the opportunity of refilling his glass, since Marvin was only playing with his—and then shifted his position in the chair as he had promised himself he would do.

All the greens in the world, he remembered. Now he saw the green of lichen, the green of fir trees, the green of ivy and the green of weeping willows in the spring.

He drank again and refilled Marvin's glass. Then he moved his chair a little and looked at the bottle once more. Obviously, it only depended on the distance of each wall-light and therefore the angle of refraction—he knew all that—but now he could definitely see the green of a drake's head, the green of

Swiss mountain pastures in summer, the green of a waterfall cascading over the rocks between banks of moss and the burgeoning green of a copse in the spring.

He reached for the bottle and refilled his glass. This, without doubt, was the most remarkable drink he had ever tasted in his life. He should remember to ask his host to give him the name and address of his farmer friend. Expensive petrol had been consumed for years at the instigation of M. le Chef, on objectives considerably less worthy....

* * * *

'It was Roche, of course, who killed her,' said Marvin suddenly. 'Either he pushed her or forced her to jump out.'

And then without any pause he continued, with not the slightest change in the inflection of his voice.

'This is a very strong liqueur, M'sieu Pinaud. It tastes very much better with coffee. I am sorry—I have so much on my mind that I completely forgot. Would you please excuse me for a few moments and I will make some.'

M. Pinaud opened his mouth to protest that it was not necessary, but Marvin was already half-way out of the door, so he closed it again and shrugged.

Then he reflected on what the other man had just said about Roche and his daughter.

When he reappeared with the coffeepot and cups and saucers on a tray he spoke to him directly.

'Look, M'sieu Marvin, I know how you feel about your daughter—but even so you cannot possibly make this accusation against Roche. It is impossible.'

Marvin lowered the coffee tray down on to the table and sat down.

'I know I am right,' he said calmly. 'She never gave me any information directly, but certain things she said and hinted turned my thoughts in that direction. And so I made enquiries about him. He is an evil man—in spite or because of his money. Did you know that he has five personal secretaries?'

'I knew he had several. The number does not surprise me.'

'All chosen for their physical attributes,

obviously, rather than for their brains. I
have spoken to the other four. And
Yvette—Yvette was one of them—poor
unhappy girl. I do not dare to think
about it—she never told me anything—
but I am convinced that his was the evi
influence—he was the cause of all her
troubles.'

He poured the coffee, black and scald-
ing hot. Then he refilled their glasses
from the bottle.'

M. Pinaud drank some and the
sipped his coffee. Marvin had been right.
Now the very taste, the aroma and the
flavour of the plums seemed to surge
through each mouthful of hot coffee and
expand in delicious sweetness, almost a
if—as if they had actually been cooking
inside him....

He laid the coffee-cup down gently in
its saucer and spoke, choosing his words
with care.

'I am inclined to agree with you,
M'sieu Marvin, that Roche is more than
likely morally responsible for the death
of your daughter. I hope to find out
more about this when I go to see him at
his office tomorrow morning.

'But in all fairness to him, you cannot accuse him of actually and physically killing her. I myself was with her until a few moments before I met you. She was alone and well when I left her and there was no one else in her flat. I took a few moments to walk to the lift. I did not hurry because I was thinking about something. No one came up to that floor. Before I left the lift the emergency alarm was already ringing, which means that the lift would have ceased to operate. The doorman must have rushed in to tell the switchboard operator. She must have jumped almost immediately after I left her—'

'But why—why—'

M. Pinaud considered for a moment. He felt that he could not talk about it now—not even to her father. What she had confessed to him had been in confidence. Again he chose his words with great care.

'I don't really know. I don't think anyone will ever know the whole truth. I would say that she had been made to suffer more than any human being could endure. It was her own choice. She was alone when she decided.'

'Yes—agreed—but who made her suffer until she could not stand any more? He did. Then why wait until to-morrow—why not go there now, both of us, and have it out with him?'

M. Pinaud looked at him with understanding and compassion.

'There are two reasons,' he replied. 'First, as I told you before in my flat, because this is my job, to deal with Roche, and not yours. It is something for which I have been trained, for many years. We cannot have odd private citizens joining in and working for the *Sûreté*—it would not be practical.

'And secondly, because Roche will not be working now at this time of the evening. And I am sure he is not the type of man to spend his evenings at home. He will be out, dining somewhere and making contacts, probably until very late. By that time I hope to be asleep. I have had a long and hard day and a knife-slash in my arm. I must rest if I am to work tomorrow.'

Marvin was immediately contrite.

'I am sorry—I did not know—'

He held up one hand.

'Of course not. I did not tell you. I can understand your eagerness—but I am sure my plan is the better one. Roche gets to work about ten o'clock at Montparnasse. I shall be there waiting for him.'

'Yes,' agreed Marvin doubtfully. For a moment he concentrated in thought. 'At least you will be able to find him. You know he will be there.'

'Exactly. Otherwise we could spend the whole of the evening looking for him.'

He stood up.

'And now, M'sieu Marvin, if you will excuse me, I feel I should be getting home. May I thank you for your courtesy and your hospitality—'

Marvin stood up as well. He seemed straighter and firmer and more composed. He interrupted with a new assurance in his voice and a very great dignity.

'That was nothing. It is I who must thank you, M'sieu Pinaud—with all my heart. I do not need words—you know what I mean. Come, I will see you out.'

As M. Pinaud walked under the clear and star-lit sky to find a taxi, he remembered that he had eaten nothing that day. It was fortunate that there was still plenty of stew left in the saucepan.

CHAPTER 12

Janice Arnaud was upset. What was more, she made no attempt to hide it, not even from that dashing, virile and potential lunch-buyer, Hector Lebrun.

'Your appointment, M'sieu Lebrun, was for yesterday morning and not for today. Was it you who telephoned about half an hour ago?'

'No. I am extremely sorry but—'

'And what is more, it was for eleven o'clock and not ten—'

'I can explain. You see, it was—'

'You must understand that M'sieu Roche is a very dedicated and madly busy man. He has vast interests—projects with enormous ramifications—operations involving gigantic profits. A broken appointment—'

'Look, Madame Arnaud—'

In spite of her upset, she tried gallantly to summon a smile.

'The name is still Janice—you must

have forgotten,' she said demurely. It might have been such a wonderful and thrilling friendship. But even as she tried she knew that she had failed.

As she recounted to her girl-friend that evening—it was hopeless—almost frightening—he seemed like a different man—like a tiger waiting to spring—I tell you he looked right through me—although with our lunch in mind I was still wearing this new lace blouse for another day—and never even saw anything at all—and yet he was so quiet and sad at the same time—I tell you it made me shiver all over—just to look at him—

The realization of failure gave her even more eloquence. The words poured out in a torrent.

'I don't know what is happening to the world today nor to the people in it—no wonder I am upset—I was just opening M'sieu Roche's office at nine-thirty punctually as I always do when they came to fetch me from the next office down the corridor—contracts and legal —to say that I was wanted on the telephone—their extension number is the next one to mine—and would I mind going in there to take it as it would be quicker than trying to connect the call back through the switchboard which is always busy and engaged at that time in the morning—so I rushed out and down there leaving all the doors open and I would not have minded if it had been anything sensible or important but as soon as I spoke he hung up and I got the dialling tone—would you believe it, M'sieu Lebrun—'

M. Pinaud decided then that he had heard enough of this nonsense and took out his credentials. His voice was quiet and impersonal.

'Not Lebrun, Madame Arnaud. I am Pinaud of the *Sûreté*. I apologize for the deception the other day, but it was necessary and of vital importance. Now I have official business with M'sieu Roche as soon as he arrives. He is due in at ten o'clock, I understand?'

She nodded, unable to speak, seemingly hypnotized by his card and badge.

'Good. I will wait in his office there with the door open. Answer the telephone if it rings, but no outgoing calls, please.'

Again she did not answer. He crossed over the room, opened the door of Roche's office, left it open and went inside.

* * * *

Roche arrived shortly afterwards. By that time Janice Arnaud had recovered her voice.

'Good morning, m'sieu,' she said softly and sweetly. And then, louder for M. Pinaud's benefit:

'A M'sieu Pinaud from the *Sûreté* is waiting in your office. He claims to have official business with you.'

Roche did not answer. He walked straight into his office and closed the door behind him. He threw his hat on to a chair and sat down behind his desk. His left forefinger was bandaged.

'What the devil do you want?' he asked curtly.

M. Pinaud had been standing impassively by the wall. Now he came over to the desk.

'I thought you might like to know why you have not heard from your friend

Brancard,' he replied. His voice was quiet and calmly conversational.

For a second a light seemed to glow in the heavy-lidded eyes, but it died almost as soon as it came, and the arrogant and powerful features remained impassive, brooding and calm.

'I don't know what you are talking about. M'sieu Pinaud. I have never heard of that name.'

'I thought you would take that line,' M. Pinaud told him. 'That all these things have nothing to do with you. This would be your protection if anything went wrong. I am pleased to be able to tell you, M'sieu Roche, that everything did go wrong with your operation. The traitor Brancard is dead and we have the barge and the heroin.'

Still the impassive features betrayed no emotion.

'You are wasting my time,' Roche told him.

For a long moment there was silence. When M. Pinaud spoke his voice had changed. It was still quiet, but subtly harder, and cold with a frightening undertone of menace.

'You have heard about Yvette Rostand?'

The reply came without hesitation.

'Yes. On the early-morning news.'

'You killed her.'

'Nonsense. She threw herself out from the balcony.'

'I know—but why?'

'Why does any stupid woman—'

'She was not stupid. She was unhappy. She was so unhappy she no longer wished to live. You started her on drugs—yours is the responsibility. When Henri Rostand would not agree to your schemes you deliberately destroyed his marriage by seducing his wife and making her your accomplice to get rid of him.'

He paused for a moment, but Roche did not speak.

'Have you ever thought about what would have happened to your cargo of heroin afterwards—after you had made your money out of it? Of the crime and the degradation and the broken lives that always go with addiction? Have you thought of the children in schools who are being taught the habit? It seems to me, M'sieu Roche, that your responsi-

bility is almost beyond human understanding.'

He ceased to speak and again there
was a silence between them.

Then Roche laughed. So might one of
his ancestors have laughed as he reclined
beneath the awnings of purple and gold,
sipping his goblet of iced Falernian wine
and pointing his thumb downwards, towards the golden and blood-soaked sand
of the arena....

It was an inhuman sound. M. Pinaud
imagined that a cold hand was clutching
at his heart.

'You should have been a priest, not a
detective,' Roche jeered. 'You may be
good at preaching sermons—but you will
find that proving any of this nonsense is
another matter. How are you going to
prove anything? Have you come here to
arrest me?'

M. Pinaud shook his head slowly.

'No. Your money and your influence
would be able to buy the best lawyers in
the country—and even perhaps some of
the judges. You are right. I have no
proof. All the witnesses are dead.'

His eyes still watched the other man,

but behind him he saw them all and the manner in which they had died. And as he continued to speak, his voice now was soft and sad.

'But I believe that a marriage is a sacred thing. You have proved that your views are different. What you tried to do to me, because I stood in your way, was in the same class of sick and perverted thinking—something I can never under-stand nor forgive. Mercifully you failed But with Yvette Rostand you succeeded.

Once again his voice changed. Now i became even harder than before, with the menace more clearly defined.

'There is another law, M'sieu Roche— higher than the one by which we try to live. You may not have heard of it—you worship only money.'

'What do you mean?'

The words were little more than a whisper. For the first time Roche showed emotion. For the first time in his life he was afraid. This deadly quietness, this supreme assurance, this ruthless implaca bility—these were all things he had never encountered before.

The tension between them mounted

until it seemed almost palpable, almost physical.

'Men have evolved a code of laws for thousands of years, ever since they came out of the jungle to build—in order to contain people like you. But even after such experience, there are sometimes situations for which the law has no remedy. Then there is another law—a higher one. I do not pretend to understand it myself. I only know that not once but many times I have seen its manifestations, and therefore I must believe in it. One does not have to understand to believe, M'sieu Roche. There are things called faith and trust—qualities we all have as children and lose so easily as we grow up.'

* * * *

In the silence that followed he pointed to the exquisitely chased silver box which still lay on the desk.

'Open it.'

This was a command, hard and incisive.

Roche made no move to obey. He

shook his head.

'No.'

The next instant there was a gun in M. Pinaud's hand. Roche never knew how. He saw the hand move, with incredible speed, and then the gun was there, aiming at his heart.

'Open it,' I said.'

With his right hand Roche reached out across the desk and opened the box. The small automatic was still inside.

'Lift it out, put it back in the box and close the lid.'

Roche did so.

Now the commands were ended. Now that quiet and deadly voice addressed him again.

'You are a man who could kidnap a mother and her children for the sake of money. I knew even then that we were bound to meet again. Something told me to choose your left finger and not the right when I came here last to get my children back. At the time I did not know why. Now I do. Even then the decision must have been made. This is what I was trying to explain about that higher law—very often it is hard to understand how every action is co-ordinated to achieve a purpose. This time I can see it all very clearly.'

'What are you saying?'

The words were hardly articulate. It was a hoarse whisper broken with terror.

The quiet sad voice had no mercy.

'I mean that your automatic will be found beside your dead hand with your fingerprints all over it. You tried to shoot me with a gun concealed in a box on your desk, resisting arrest. I would have been entitled to fire in self-defence.'

* * * *

The cloakroom door opened inwards, so quietly that he knew it must have been ajar, and out of the corners of his eyes he saw Victor Marvin step into the office.

'I told you last night—' he began, with for the first time a note of strain in his voice. He did not dare to take his attention from Roche, who was moving stealthily now in his chair, as tense as a tiger about to spring.

'I know you did,' interrupted Marvin quietly, 'but you were wrong. I am sorry, but you were completely wrong. You told me that this was your job. I have been listening behind that door, which was not shut, ever since that—that animal came in. What I heard convinced me more than ever that I was right. This is my job and not yours.'

'How did you get in?' asked M. Pinaud, still without taking his eyes from Roche.

'It was easy. I asked a friend of mine to telephone the next extension, to get Madame Arnaud out of her office so that I could slip in here without being seen.'

Marvin began to walk towards them, slowly and deliberately. As he came beside the desk he suddenly flung out one hand and with astonishing speed and dexterity snatched up the silver cigarette box.

'He is desperate now,' he said, 'and will take any risk. I will put this out of his reach.'

Without pausing in his stride, he went on past the desk towards the opposite wall, where M. Pinaud remembered there was a heavy armchair. He could no longer see him, because Marvin was now behind his range of vision.

He still faced Roche, all his attention concentrated on the man seated at his desk. In some strange way, he thought, it was as if they had never been interrupted, as though Marvin had never entered the room. There were only the two of them left in the whole world, bound and held captive by the awful tension his last words had created.

Suddenly the room seemed to split with a blinding pain in the back of his head and he felt a frenzied grip over his own hand holding the gun. Faintly through his swimming senses, as he fell to his knees, he heard the sound of a shot.

* * * *

The carpet seemed to be heaving under his hands and his head was throbbing from his skull to his eyes, but he did not lose consciousness.

Faintly, in a macabre synchronization with the throbbing in his head, he heard a knocking on the office door. And he heard the echoes, softly through the sound-proofing, of what Madame Arnaud was probably shouting to say.

He forced himself up with a supreme effort, fighting to ignore the pain and the throbbing. Afterwards—when all this was over—perhaps he could lie down and rest. But not now—not now.

He felt Marvin's arm beneath his own, helping him, almost lifting him to his feet, and heard his anxious whisper:

'Are you all right, M'sieu Pinaud? I had to use the box—but I did not hit you hard.'

Summoning all his strength, he tore Marvin's arm away and waved him violently to the near corner of the room, where he would not be seen with the door open.

Then he forced himself—he never afterwards could tell how—to walk to the door. Every second was vital now—before she gave up shouting and went to summon other people. He opened it and stood on the threshold.

'M'sieu Roche—M'sieu Roche—'

After that one hoarse whisper Madame Arnaud had neither breath nor words left.

'I am sorry to have to tell you that there has been an accident,' he told her quickly. 'Would you please wait here just a few moments longer and then I shall ask you inside as a witness. Then you will have to telephone the police and an ambulance. Meanwhile—until I send for you—do not touch the telephone or allow anyone into your office. That is an order.'

Then he closed the door and drew the bolt quietly. His mind was rapidly clearing, perhaps because of the effort he had made, and the pain was now definitely less acute.

He walked to the desk. His gun lay on its polished surface, the butt towards him, beside the silver box, once again in its usual place. The body of Roche sprawled on the carpet beside his overturned chair.

'Is he dead?' he asked.

'Yes—through the heart. He was not fit to live.'

Marvin came to join him as he replied.

'He tried to leap from the chair as soon as I hit you, but I was ready for him,' he continued quietly. 'My hand was over yours on the gun. You know where I live, M'sieu Pinaud. I shall not run away.'

For one brief and unforgettable moment he stood there, as M. Pinaud was always to remember him in the years to come, a sad but no longer a pathetic figure, an old man crowned with a strange and wonderful dignity, a man who had taken the law into his own hands for the sake of his principles and who in consequence seemed to stand both tall and proud.

'I loved my daughter,' he continued, speaking very softly. 'I loved her in the days of her childhood, when we were happy together, and I loved her even more when I saw the ruin she had made of her life. This thing had to be done—for her sake.'

M. Pinaud swiftly opened the silver box and without touching the automatic, tipped it out on to the carpet next to Roche's outflung right hand. Then he replaced the box, with its lid open on the desk in front of where Roche had sat. Finally he took Marvin by the arm.

'Stand behind the door,' he said quietly. 'I will bring her straight in to the desk so that she does not turn around. That will be your only chance. Out through her office. If anyone speaks to you in the corridor, say you had an appointment with me in Roche's office.'

And he held out his hand.

* * * *

Then he went to the door and opened it half-way.

'Would you please come in now, Madame Arnaud,' he told her.

She had recovered her breath and her speech, but she had no tears for her late employer. After all, men come and go— Madame Arnaud instead of Janice told her clearly that she had almost certainly lost this promising one as well—but it was a well-known fact that there were more fish in the sea than ever came out.

And besides, she was far too excited at the importance of her new role—imagine my dear, an actual witness for the *Sûreté*, I tell you I saw his badge—and far too busy already composing the epic narrative her girl-friend would hear that night to shed tears over what had really never been anything more than the other —but very necessary—end of a commercial transaction.

He marched her straight across the room at a fast pace to the desk, keeping his body behind her shoulder in case she should turn her head. But she had eyes only for the scene in front of her.

'We had sufficient evidence to convict your employer of complicity in trafficking in heroin,' he told her. 'I came here to arrest him. He suddenly snatched a gun from that silver box on the desk and would have shot me if I had not fired first. The official inquiry and inquest should be just routine procedure, but I brought you in here, Madame Arnaud, in case we should need a reliable and independent witness. Would you please note the position of the body—I was standing here—the box on the desk, and his gun, an automatic, on the carpet where it fell out of his hand. That is my own gun on the desk.'

'Yes—oh yes. It is all quite clear.'

'Right. Now would you be kind enough to go back to your office and send out an emergency call for the police and an ambulance. I shall join you in a moment. Thank you very much.'

He had remembered to check his gun and cover it with his own fingerprints while re-loading the one cartridge fired. He had remembered to wipe the silver box very carefully, press the dead man's fingerprints all over it and replace it, using his clean handkerchief, on the desk with the lid open.

Now he sat down wearily in the armchair, waiting for the police. The pain in his head had subsided to a dull ache. The thoughts came swooping through his mind like birds on the wing.

Victor Marvin had suffered enough. He could not add to such a burden. But to him it would make no difference. All it meant was another entry in his report, a different final page to the file, another unanswerable question added to M. le Chef's already complicated opinion of him and the case brought to a satisfactory conclusion.

Marvin had been right. Such men were not fit to live. And if they had arrested him he would have laughed and been acquitted. They had no proof, no evidence. All the witnesses were dead.

And what would have happened if Marvin had not opened the cloakroom door? He knew that in spite of all his words he could never have brought himself to kill a man in cold blood. He knew that he dared not think about the man's execution too much, because this was the one occasion on which he might well have taken the responsibility himself...

Now, as if cradled on a wave of release from those moments of almost unbearable tension, he knew that mercifully he did not have to think at all. The thinking had been taken from out of his mind. His problem had ceased to exist. Another and higher power had solved it for him. The sequence of events had been complicated and yet logical enough to understand. He had tried to explain to Roche with what he knew was pitiful inadequacy, but to him the working of the law, as it had always been from so many other maifestations, was completely clear.

He stood up and walked out of that room, silent now with the presence of death.

He walked slowly, sad with the pity

and the horror and the tragedy of it all. He walked with humility, once again awed at the majesty of a power that could so control his life. And he walked with thankfulness, in recognition of the mercy he had been shown...

THE SAINT TITLES
IN LARGE PRINT

The Saint in New York

The Saint v. Scotland Yard

The Saint and Mr. Teal

The Saint and the
People Importers

The Saint and the
Hapsburg Necklace

Catch the Saint

The Saint Abroad

WILBUR SMITH TITLES
IN LARGE PRINT

Goldmine

The Diamond Hunters

Eagle in the Sky. (two volumes)

The Eye of The Tiger. (two volumes)

When the Lion Feeds. (two volumes)

The Dark Of The Sun

Shout At The Devil

The Sound of Thunder